The Great Beyond

Keith Allan Shields

CONTENTS

Preface

A great many people have written of heaven and hell and I am indebted to more of them than I might realize. It is hard to say how much Dante's perspective may have affected me since his influence upon general culture is unclear. I know that other authors have certainly influenced me in the writing of this short novel. C.S. Lewis, George MacDonald (particularly his brilliant short-story, "The Grey Wolf"), Rudyard Kipling, and a host of poets, song-writers, and dreamers have influenced the words you will read in this book.

The Great Beyond is a metaphor and is open to interpretation. It is not an attempt at theological explanations of the afterlife. My hope is that it might encourage thoughtfulness toward spiritual realities and the hope of heaven. *The Great Beyond* is also an attempt to paint pictures in the mind. My hope is that the images might inspire readers to wonder about the nature of our universe, the physical world, and the spiritual world.

Acknowledgements and Thanks

The words of the wise are like cattle prods—
painful but helpful. Their collected sayings
are like a nail-studded stick with which a
shepherd drives the sheep.
But, my child, let me give you some further
advice: Be careful, for writing books is
endless, and much study wears you out.
That's the whole story. Here now is my final
conclusion: Fear God and obey his
commands, for this is everyone's duty. God
will judge us for everything we do, including
every secret thing, whether good or bad. —
Ecclesiastes 12:11-14 (New Living
Translation)

Many wise words from many authors and
many books have contributed to the writing of
this book. I am thankful to teachers who
encouraged me to read and write from a young
age.
  I am thankful for my children who listened as I
read them classics like *The Chronicles of Narnia*
and *The Lord of the Rings*.
  The final editor for this work was Tara Miller.
Her expert advice made the final product much
better.
  Thanks to Tyler Williams of Heard
Communications, who did the cover design.
  My wife, Maureen, has been my constant
encourager and my first editor

1. The End

The weightlessness of the moment caught him by surprise. Ray could see his arms flailing as his body rotated and his feet drifted toward the sky. The sun glinted off something near his toe. It wasn't as if he could take all of this in, but he had a sense that he had entered a slow-motion replay of his bodily contortions. Ray had time to see the motions, experience the nausea caused by the forces upon his body, and trace the moments that had led to the present experience. He thought about the drive out to the secluded well-site and how he knew he had been driving too fast, daring some young RCMP officer to flag him down and send him home with a ticket. He sensed the gravel shifting and flowing with the weight and speed of his truck. The dust blew across the fields and tracked his progress to the place to which he was drawn. The emotions of leaving things behind and racing toward something he should have wanted to avoid hung heavy like the dust in the air at sunset. Why had he been in such a hurry?

There were many things that were not making sense right now. The weightlessness seemed to go on long after the motion of truck and gravel had been brought to rest by gravity and time. His body, which should have been held down by seatbelt and truck cab, was in a slow drift toward the sky that was beginning to be populated with a myriad of stars. How could he continue to fly for so long? He thought he remembered bringing the truck to rest at a little cliff overlooking a slough and a pump-jack. Did he fall? Why did it seem that he was falling upward? The tricks of light reflecting off the pond transitioned into stars and he was aware of the passage of time as he fell unescapably into the void between him and them. He was a voyager, separated from time and space, drifting through the far reaches of the cosmos toward an orbit around some distant star. He marvelled that his lungs could breathe in and breathe out without assistance.

But the journey was yet in his control. Through gentle movements of head and toes, he could change the trajectory. An arm thrust one direction moved him in a line toward Polaris; toes pointed and head swivelled in another direction made Venus appear to be his destination. Somersaults and barrel-rolls were fair game and changed his direction accordingly. "Where to now?" was the message his brain sent out to the listening universe at the end of the first day.

2. Space

"Day" became a figurative term. Ray began to measure time in intervals which may or may not have approximated 24-hour periods on earth. Each new "day" seemed to have new possibilities and new adventures. Day two started that way. He saw a bright light in the distance which seemed to him to be the planet Venus. He remembered finding it on a star chart and showing it to a granddaughter in a time and place prior to whatever this was. The bright and morning star it had been called. It had a vaguely religious association to it and he wondered why that would be. He looked at the planet with two conflicting emotions at war within him. The light seemed appealing and welcoming, a bright sunny place where he might rest awhile. At the same time, his mind was filled with a loathing as if the place held an entity he was not yet prepared to meet. It seemed as if a great monster were there waiting for him to dare to set foot on his world so that Ray might be consumed, flesh, spirit, bone and all by the horrific beast. Should he head in that direction or not? If not in that direction, then where? For the better part of the day he chose a path that took him a good distance away from the bright, morning star and instead toward a place of great blackness. He wanted to get away from the bright light of Venus and strike out on a path that seemed less contrived, less scripted for him by someone else. For hours, or days, or years, he drifted at his constant speed. He could not tell if it was extremely rapid or immeasurably slow. There were no points of reference to give him a sense of time, speed, or his place in the solar system.

Drifting through space left a lot of time for contemplating life. He began to think about his granddaughter, the one who had looked at the star chart with him. His heart began to ache with the loneliness of rejection and estrangement. She would be about 12 years old now, but he still thought of her as the four-year-old she had been when he last saw her. She was clever; even at four years old she could understand the difference between a planet and a star. Why had he let his son take her away from him? Why had they said he was a bad influence on her and denied him access to her? Sure, he drank a bit but that was the life of hard-working factory labourers. Work hard, play hard, drink hard, and then sober up for the next day of work. It was also how he numbed the pain of the losses in his life. He forcefully changed the subject of his contemplations. His mind went where it usually did in times like these: back to Lydia, that remarkable bartender at the Wicklow Pub. Oh, if only... but his thoughts trailed off and he began to think of other destinations.

It seemed to Ray that he was neither getting any closer to the black spot toward which he had aimed nor further away from the bright light of Venus. It was taking so long to get anywhere that he felt time and space were frozen and nothing would ever change if he did not do something. Finally, he chose to move closer to Venus and set his aim toward that objective.

Immediately, the universe sped up. Whether he had been going fast or slow before, he was now moving faster than anything he could imagine. If indeed the distant star was Venus, and if he had started back at planet Earth, the speed with which he arrived must have been greater than the speed of light. He soon found himself drawing very close to warmth and bordering a cloud enshrouded planet. The colour was, at points, orange like a creamsicle, at other points blue like an ocean, and still further on, green like a tiger's eye. He realized that for some time now he had been racing through shards of clouds that encased a planet made almost entirely of ocean. It was just as his brain began to make sense of the fact that he was falling, now in the appropriate direction, toward a surface that was rising rapidly to meet him, that he hit with a large splash into a deep ocean. He must have travelled downward through the blue-green fluid for several hours before slowing to a stop and then, at first, rising slowly from the depths until racing at break-neck speed toward the surface. When he got there, he breached out of the water like a frolicking gray whale and rocketed so far above the surface of the water that he thought he might be once again thrown out into space. Yet he soon fell back toward sea level on the Venusian surface where he eventually came to a halt, bobbing like an apple in the crystal seas. Not a speck of land was visible and he wondered for a moment if he might be there until he drowned. Then he thought about his strange means of locomotion through space that had not been difficult and was again struck by the curious nature of his circumstances.

As he began to wonder what to do next, the world went from bright day to dim dusk to darkest night in a few short minutes. Ray could see a dark layer of clouds above his head and knew that there must be stars beyond but he could not see them. Darkness fell even blacker and he must have slept in this most luxurious waterbed.

He awoke at sunrise with the sound of sea birds in his ears, as if he had heard them in his sleep or dreams, but saw no evidence of any such life. He was alone in the world still. Far off on the horizon he began to make out a shape. The shape was rather indistinct. Was it an outcropping of land? An island? A peninsula of some great land mass? A boat? A being like himself drifting on the surface of the sea? He could not tell. What he could see was that it was getting closer to him. Or was he getting closer to it? Either case could be true.

As the two grew closer and closer, he was aware of the steady current of the liquid beneath him. He could not yet bring himself to call this liquid water, for it tasted sweeter than water, was tropical in temperature, and had not the slightest hint of salt. Nor had he seen any living thing in the sea. No fish, no minnows, no weeds, no plankton, and certainly no mammals. Could it be water and be this sterile? But now as he drew ever closer to the object on the horizon, the liquid became alive. First a few cells that looked like large bacteria or small plant life began to drift by; then a few strands of weedy-looking kelp; then larger bits of plant life; followed by the smallest of shrimplike creatures with limbs, tentacles, and feelers spread around their perimeter. Next came little fish followed by larger fish, and then sharks and barracudas, and turtles. Lastly, a great herd of whales, dolphins, and the largest seahorses he had ever seen came streaming by. The entire zoo of plant and animal life was whirling past him, over him, under him, to his left, to his right and everywhere until he felt like the very sea was boiling and alive with more creatures than could possibly fit in this much ocean. Some of the life around him looked familiar. Some was so exotic as to appear to be part of a dream. Some sort of cow with an udder and tail went swimming by as gracefully as a dolphin. In fact, its head looked like that of a dolphin except that it had the horns of a bovine sticking out of the top of its head. Not once did Ray fear for his life or expect to get punctured by a passing horn. Despite their speed and proximity, every member of the swarm knew its place in the sea and could not possibly crash into or obstruct another living beast or plant. All was in order and perfectly synchronized.

He noticed that some of the plants appeared to be saying something to him. Then he realized that it was absurd for sea vegetables to be talking just as he realized that the animals were also speaking. He could not understand a word. Each bark, squeal, growl, whinny, splash, and gurgle was absolutely intelligible to someone, but just not to him. A thousand languages were being spoken around him and all Ray could hear was gibberish. Yet, at one and the same time, his mind was being flooded with the sense that he was supposed to pull up his feet, curl into a ball and tuck his head as low as possible. He had just acquired this position when the surf threw him onto a sandy beach and his body rolled at hundreds of kilometers per hour over kilometers of beach for an hour or more before coming to rest in a heap of grass. Not one of the sea creatures or plants ended up with him. He was alone with a whole new menagerie of birds, monkeys, worms, snakes, snails, mice, crickets, squirrels, tiger-headed chimpanzees, moose-headed rats, and parakeets with an extra set of appendages holding seeds and stuffing them in their beaks. Again, it felt like far too many creatures for the space in which everything resided. He sat sprawled on the grass beneath a large umbrella tree which had lately caused his rolling motion to stop. He was no worse for wear and he could not find a single bruise or tender spot anywhere on his body. He laughed at his present state of mind and the unusual world in which he had landed.

What was this world? Ray had never been very religious. He had not spent a lot of time thinking about heaven and hell, but what was this place? Was this some sort of life after life? Was this heaven? Was this hell? He remembered the debates back in that other world before this one. Could there be life after death? Could there be life on other planets? Had God created life in just six days? What about dinosaurs? What about science and evolution? These arguments and many others had often been a source of entertainment for Ray. He had no horse in the race and he didn't care how the argument went. He loved to rile up the guys in the lunchroom at work and set the circus in motion. Once he got things started, he would sit back and watch the fun. He knew all the acts that would follow. One of his atheist friends would make disparaging comments about those who could still believe in a God that made a man from dirt, put him to sleep, and took out one of his ribs to make a woman. He would say that it was the same as Viking sailors calling upon the gods of the storms to protect them from drowning, and sacrificing one of the lesser warriors to appease the gods. One of the Bible-toters would then say that the creation story in Genesis was the story that made more sense than all the rest. A science-loving buddy would remind them all that they could not trust in any fairy-tales and that empirical measurement was all that would stand up to scrutiny: "If it can't be measured, seen, heard, or touched, it doesn't exist." He would speak of the tree of life that had been uncovered by the study of genetics. He would point to Neanderthals and Apes and common ancestors of man. A Bible-toter would try to blend science and the Bible together and explain how it all fit. Once the carnival had been set in motion, nothing could bring it to conclusion except running out of break time. Ray knew it all, had heard it all, could quote all sides of the debate. Sometimes he changed the part that he played, just to keep it interesting. The arguments seemed so unimportant now. Here he was in some place with more varieties of life than he could imagine, on some planet that wasn't supposed to have life. He was in some alternate reality and had gotten here without need of a spacecraft or even a breathing apparatus. This had to be a spiritual reality, but what did that mean? Was it all a dream? Was this an alternate universe? An alternate reality? Was there a God behind all of this? Ray had too little information to make sense of it all. Night fell again and his mind was asleep and unaware.

3. Unwelcome

Morning on the fourth day, third day? twelfth day? broke with rolling clouds and excessive humidity. Most of the wildlife was gone and he sat alone under the tree with an occasional twitter from a bird in a far-off tree. Ray began to wonder what he should do next, when he heard the sounds of habitation. Someone was chopping at something with what sounded like an axe. He looked in the direction of the sound and saw some movement through the trees. He began to move in the direction of the sound and movement. As he drew closer he could see a man using a machete to hack out a section of roof on a small grass-roofed hut. The walls were made of rough sticks, twigs, and branches with vines woven through to hold them together. The man who clung to the roof was doing repairs and filling in a hole that had developed in his roof. As he worked he seemed to be muttering to himself and cursing someone who had caused this destruction to his home. His complexion and features looked distinctly British but his hair was plaited in dreadlocks and his face was painted garishly like one who has prepared to go to war. He was not yet aware that Ray was approaching and Ray could hear him speaking as if to someone by his side. "So, they think they can drive me away that easily do they? Hah! I will show them! Take away my roof, will they? I hate them all. All I want is to be left alone. Do ya hear me, ya evil swine?" With these and a great many other words, the man lifted curses to the skies as if a large audience were hearing his complaints. Ray could not see any evidence of persons, swine, or anything that might be responsible for damages done to the hut and so he pressed closer.

Ray stepped forward and began to greet the man. Instantly, the man leapt down from the roof and brandished the machete in his direction. "Ha! There you are, you despicable slug! So, you have come back to gloat over your accomplishments, have you? I ought to cut you in half where you stand! And I will if you don't get away from here real quick, you surly excuse for a man." The crazed look in the eyes of the man was enough to scare Ray, but he thought he should try to explain that he had just arrived in this country and he couldn't possibly be responsible for the man's hardships. Speaking as quickly as he could manage, he tried to pacify the man, but he would not be deterred. In the mind of this crazed man, Ray was the only person around, and so he must be the one who had damaged his home. Ray narrowly missed a swing of the blade and tried once again to explain and calm the man. He would not be calmed. Ray dodged a few more parries of the machete and realized that the whole thing was a hopeless cause. He could not reason with this strange, crazed, isolated man.

Ray decided the only reasonable solution was to get away. He moved off hastily through the jungle. He could hear the man screaming curses behind him, calling down every kind of disease and injury imaginable upon Ray. Ray was not in great physical shape, but in this place, with such motivation, he did not stop jogging for several hours.

4. The Collector

Ray was once again lost in his thoughts as he walked a solitary road. His attention turned to Evelyn, his granddaughter. Such an old-fashioned name for a young girl. He wondered where she was right now. Maybe she was at school. Maybe she was asleep in her bed. If it was Sunday morning, he knew that she and her parents would be sitting in church. It gave Ray a sense of peace to think about them sitting there and interacting with their friends at church. When she was little, Evie had loved her classroom at the church. She wanted Ray to come with her to church and see the picture on the wall in that room. Ray had even gone in once to see the large mural of Jesus sitting among a crowd of children.

His son, Ray Jr., or Junie, as he liked to be called, had not always been religious. Ray had raised him up to be a tough-guy. Ray knew that the world was big and hard and would beat him down if Ray Jr. didn't show some strength. He didn't want anyone walking over his son. He taught him to box and never back down from a fight. He taught him to drink when he was fourteen so that his first experience of being drunk wouldn't be with his friends. It turned out that Ray Jr. had less of a tolerance for alcohol than his father. There had been some bad years when Junie dropped out of school and got into other things besides booze. Ray had repeatedly warned him to stay away from that stuff. Why hadn't Junie listened?

Junie was certainly on a better road now. Ray didn't know about this religion thing, but at least his son had kicked his habits and gone back to school. He heard that he was doing well as an electrical engineer. His wife was plain but had a way of showing love to everyone and every creature. She found it hard to kill the mice that sometimes invaded their home on the acreage. Ray wondered what he might have done to get to know Junie, Joanna, and Evelyn better. He realized now that he should have at least tried. Was it too late now? His mind came back to the place in which he found himself and answered his own question, "Yes, I guess it is too late now."

When next he was aware of his surroundings, Ray became conscious of the fact that he had been moving slowly up a small incline and just now the incline was getting steep. He looked down at his feet and saw that the vines and soil over which he walked were matted together with shells, bits of metal, bones, carved sticks, wire, bits of food, cooking utensils, and various other items. As he moved more slowly forward he could see that he was climbing to the top of an ancient mound. The closer he got to the top, the newer the items and the less embedded in soil. It took him most of a day to climb close to the top and when he got to the very peak, he could not help but think that someone or some people must have spent a very long time creating this gigantic mound. He did not have long to think about it for as he looked down the mound on the other side, he heard a horrible shriek and saw a person racing up the mound on a large but silent motorcycle with sidecar and trailer. The two attachments connected to the motorcycle were packed to overflowing with more of the same useless bits of stuff that made up the whole mound and it seemed that the biker had planned to bring his (or possibly her) load up but had been hastened in progress by the sight of Ray at the top of the mound. The motorcycle covered much terrain in a short period of time and soon stood on the top of the mountain of stuff. The rider leapt off before the machine had come to a stop and yelled at Ray as he stood in disbelief. The woman who stood before Ray was covered from head to toe in rings, earrings, bangles, stones, piercings, tattoos, coils of rope, metal neck-bands, branches of trees woven into basket-like clothing, and pieces of cotton cloth and wool. The woman was intimidating and, at first, Ray was frightened by her bizarre appearance. He soon realized that she posed little threat because the woman could barely move with so much stuff weighing her down. She could not raise her arms or make a fist for all the items that restricted her movements. Ray's sense of fear was quickly replaced with emotions of loathing and sadness for this person. She was terribly afraid that he might take something off the pile but was unable to do anything if he did. The desperation in her eyes was enough to cause him to despair for her sanity. He spent a few minutes calming her down and reassuring her that he was not interested in her stuff and that he would not take anything off the mound. At one point, she petted his arm, resulting in a scratchy, snaggy feeling and said, "Yes, you are a nice one. I won't bother collec - ... er hurting you. You can be on your way *now*." The force with which she said "now" betrayed more stress than she meant to reveal and Ray decided he should be on his way. He wondered how one could be so literally wrapped up in such a collection. The things she collected were, at least to him, so obviously useless and garbage-heap worthy. Couldn't she see this herself? What motivated her to collect this stuff and then go on collecting more and more of it still? As he moved down the long slope he could not hear the woman, but every time he looked over his shoulder, he could see her just a few meters behind. Her movements were silent, and had she wanted to, she might have run him over with her massive contraption. Ray felt that it was best to simply keep moving and, as anyone who has walked down a steep incline has learned, walking down this way was hard on his knees and ankles. He was completely exhausted by the time he arrived at the bottom and collapsed as darkness fell. He spent a fitful night sleeping, off and on, just beyond any of the collection, with several twigs sticking in his back or side. He was relieved when morning came and he could see the collector, far off in the distance, on the top of her mound. Perhaps it was a trick of the angle at which he was looking, but the mound appeared to have doubled in size. Ray had just the briefest fantasy about grabbing something from the pile and making a run for it, but he knew deep in his mind that the wheels of that large motorcycle would quickly pound him into the mound and he would soon become part of the collection. He decided that would be a foolhardy act. Ray moved on.

5. Mattie

As Ray trudged through the trees and pathways, the world began to open a bit more. He found himself in a sandy area with a few trees and two streams running on either side of him. He could now see farther and his eyes focussed on a structure far away on the horizon. It took him several days of solid walking but eventually he reached a large brick building with four distinct sections. Each section was topped by a turret with small windows and four different flags flew above the place. On a bench, next to one of the turrets, he surprised himself and two people. A man and a woman were absorbed in each other, kissing, hugging, and entwining around each other. They wore the most minimal of clothes and Ray was embarrassed at coming up on them quietly enough that they did not notice him until he was only about three meters away. The woman saw him first and let out a gasp before running off into the building. The man turned to Ray and asked, in shock, "Where in blazes did you come from? I haven't seen anyone in these parts in nearly a decade." Ray explained that he had most recently come from the collection mountain guarded by the motorcycle woman, but the man seemed to have no knowledge of such a place or such a woman. Ray found out that the man was named Matthew Sunday and that he no longer travelled since he had settled down here in this place with his three wives. The wives were named Monday Tuesday, Wednesday Thursday, and Friday Saturday. Matthew tried to make some joke about his Girl Friday but it was lost on Ray. Apparently, since Matthew assured Ray that it was indeed Friday, the young woman who had fled upon his arrival was named Friday. It was her day to spend time with Matthew, or Mattie, as they sometimes called him. Mattie told of how he lived in absolute bliss with his wives, but no children, here in his paradise. He said that he was indeed hopeful that he might yet find a woman for each day of the week but he was uncertain how long that might take since people now came by with less and less frequency.

He called the three women and they lined up along the bench by the side of the home. Ray was further embarrassed as he raised his eyes to these three specimens of beauty, in the most minimal of clothing, which barely covered their places of modesty. Ray felt he had never seen such beautiful women and each of them appeared to look right through his own clothing with hungry eyes. Mattie introduced each woman to Ray and whispered a description of each so that none of them could hear. Matthew pointed out that Monday was a bit on the thin side, Wednesday was near-sighted, and Friday was a bit top-heavy. But Ray had trouble seeing anything wrong with any of these women and said as much to Mattie in words that were just a little louder than he meant.

This only heightened Ray's sense that the women were hungering after him and he soon had a very uncomfortable feeling in his stomach. Friday began to speak in a childlike tone about how the conversation between Ray and Mattie was cutting into her time and that there would have to be "some kind of compensation" for this interruption. The other two women said that she should be glad it was Friday and to quit her whining, even as they stared at Ray. They whined to Matthew that they wanted their time with Mattie. Again, their eyes bore deep into Ray's being as if they could see his very soul. Ray wondered if he had seen a bit of drool running out of the corner of a mouth of one of these beautiful women. All three of them were clasping and unclasping their hands, twining their fingers together in a fashion that suggested they wished to strangle something.

Matthew told them all to shut up or they'd all be locked up in their towers. Mattie had begun to get a sense that this newcomer might be more of a problem than the distraction was worth. He sent the women off into the house and they went away like dogs that had been scolded by their master, looking over their shoulders at Ray, and with their eyes, begging him to follow. Ray longed to give in and do just that.

Matthew tried once again to strike up a conversation with Ray. He spoke of a fishing trip he had taken many years ago, back when he still liked to fish. Matthew seemed to find the story fascinating and amusing, but Ray could not follow it nor did he find anything of interest in the story. After a long fishing story followed by the stories of how he had acquired each of his wives, and a story about a place that existed only in Mattie's dreams, Ray was about to move on when Matthew asked him for a story from his life. Mattie said he was a collector of stories, dreams, and fantasies. Ray began to tell a story of the dreams he had had to be a good father and the plans he had for his son, surprisingly deep discussions considering that the two had just met. But Matthew soon was bored with the story and told Ray that he needed to go; it was almost dark and Friday would wonder where he was. No sooner had Mattie moved off into the house than darkness snapped tight over the entire surroundings. Ray could not see where anything was and so he simply lay on the bench that was there before him and quickly fell asleep. His dreams were full of the howling of wolves, visions of teeth, claws, and blood. Once he woke in the night and thought he felt the brush of fur against his shoulder and heard a low snarl. His heart pounded and he wondered if he would survive the night, but he quickly returned to sleep and more restless dreams.

Morning came as quickly as night, as if someone had switched on a light or snapped open a blind. Ray found that the house had moved nearly a kilometer away from the bench on which he lay. He was both drawn to and repulsed by the thought of going toward the house and so he splashed in a stream for an hour before he made his way toward the house. Now it seemed that the house was at least three kilometers away. When he finally arrived, he found that all the windows and doors were tightly barred and even the glass had been covered with something dark and impenetrable. He knocked and cried out to Matthew and even used the names of the women but received no response. Seeing no way to be welcomed in and no means of forceful entry, Ray made his way down what appeared to be a faint pathway, or was it the remains of a dry creek bed? The brick house was just beginning to pass out of sight and mind when he thought he heard a feminine voice call his name, but the end of the word was cut off and lost in the wind. Ray continued on his way.

6. Sugar

The interaction with the women brought to mind Ray's ex-wife. They had been so young when they got together and very quickly Caroline was pregnant. They thought buying a couple of left-hand rings and tying the knot was the only answer, but they were so different: he was rough and blue-collar; she was refined and from a wealthy family. On a whim, she and her girlfriends had decided to go to that cowboy bar on the other side of town where she met Ray. He made her laugh and she thought that was all she needed, but it wasn't enough and soon they were arguing and even throwing things at each other.

Ray had tried hard to smooth things over with Caroline many times. He thought of the time he had jetted her away to Paris for an anniversary trip. Her parents were a little too pleased to take care of Ray Jr. and Ray wondered if Junior would return to him as a Bible-thumping, six-day creation, mouth-breather, but he was willing to take the chance for the sake of the marriage. He could recall the café in Paris where they drank espresso and Americanos from cups with handles too tiny for his fingers. They laughed as they each took turns at spilling coffee on Caroline's spy novel. They had taken the train to Rome and been baffled by the rituals and practises of Catholics. They had laughed at the red lipstick marks on the statues of Jesus, some in rather embarrassing spots, and wondered about the stories of paintings that cried real tears. Ray thought about how they should have gone to Vegas instead of Europe. The Vegas strip had an Eiffel Tower, didn't it? They travelled back to Paris and Ray discovered a wine that he liked. He drank too much, couldn't sleep, went walking the streets after midnight, and nearly got himself arrested. Caroline had thrown her book at him when he returned in the early hours of the morning. Ray yanked the phone cable out of the wall and the anniversary reconciliation was lost.

By the time Ray Jr. was five years old, the marriage was over. They were sleeping in different beds in the same house and trying to act like they still cared. They lived that way for 20 years, until one day Caroline just disappeared. Junie was having a rough time right then and Ray knew she didn't want to have anything to do with an alcoholic husband and a coke-head son. Ray still didn't know where she was. Her family hated him – they always had. If they knew where she was they sure kept it hidden. Tears formed in his eyes as Ray thought about the beautiful woman Caroline had been. He knew he had made her life a living hell. He felt ashamed as he walked along. He focused on nothing but his shoes for the next while.

He had not gone far before he saw an unusual tree. Ray was used to seeing trees that had seeds, or blossoms, or fruit, or brightly coloured leaves, but this tree had all those things at the same time. In fact, it looked like it had two types of fruit, a dark woody type, like a nut, and a soft fleshy type, almost like a pear. The blossoms were mostly pink with a few yellow mixed in. Both colours looked fully developed and the petals were about ten by ten centimeters. There were thick, solid roots that ran just below the surface of the surrounding soil and thin air roots that reached up a meter in the air before plunging back down into the soil. Ray could readily see that some of the roots had been broken off and perhaps chewed by some animal. Some of the nuts and fruits were obviously missing from a few of the low branches. It looked like the tree had become a banqueting table for someone or some animal.

Ray was just about to reach out and try one of the nuts. He did not yet feel hungry, but the fruit and nuts were appealing in their own way. He was stopped by a sound he heard on the far side of the tree. As he came around he was surprised to see a young man sitting at the base of the tree. He stayed sitting and looked up with a faraway look in his eyes. The pupils of his eyes looked far too big for the irises and Ray wondered if the man was sick, but the man greeted Ray warmly and invited him to sit with him. He said his name was Kurt Osbourne but most people just called him Sugar. Ray commented on the wonderful tree upon which Sugar was leaning. Sugar said, "Yeah, ain't she a beaut? I found her here about three years ago and I haven't left her side. She gives me food, recreation, and friendship. Here try some of these nuts." Ray asked Sugar to explain what he meant and through a series of rambling attempts at explanation Ray came to understand that the tree was hallucinogenic. Every part of it could be eaten and every fruit, nut, bark, seed, root, or flower gave a different high. It became apparent that Sugar was more than a little loony from having ingested so much of this tree for so long. Sugar did not eat any materials that did not come from the tree. He spent all his days right where he sat now. Occasionally he might reach up high into the tree or even carefully climb to a low branch to get a choice blossom or seed, but he did not move from this place. Ray decided that it was a good thing that Sugar's noises had interrupted his thoughts of reaching for some of the fruit of the tree and vowed to refrain from eating anything from this unusual tree.

Sugar revelled in what he called the "glory" of his tree, and had even named the tree Gloria. He spoke of the amazing chemistry of this plant that could take sunshine, water, soil, and fertilizer and turn them into these marvelous products of photosynthesis. Where else could one find such wondrous fruits? He spoke of the "majesty" of the tree, how it had served the needs of kings and princes since the dawn of time. He was certain that this very tree had been in the Garden of Eden and had been the good fruit of which Adam and Eve had eaten. He quoted Bible verses about the herbs of the field and had memorized one he loved to recite: "And God said, 'Behold, I have given you every herb bearing seed, which is upon the face of all the earth, and every tree, in which is the fruit of a tree yielding seed; to you it shall be for meat.'"

Ray could almost see the logic in Sugar's words. Might this tree be a gift from God - or a gift from Nature (really, what was the difference?). He could smell the blossoms in the high branches and the pungent aroma made him think of fine wines and delicious foods. Ray realized he had not had anything to eat for many days. Could this be the place where that provision was being made for him? He could not say that these feelings were physical hunger. He had not experienced that need in this world, but neither did he feel satisfied. There was a hungering in a place he could not identify. It was not exactly in his stomach, nor was it in his brain or his heart. Ray began to question his sanity again. What were all these thoughts about heart, brain, and stomach? Ray had never been much of a philosopher.

But Ray also knew the joy of good food, good drink, and good intoxication. The aroma of the seeds beside his head was starting to appeal to his mind. It was as if this tree was calling out to him, asking him to trust these feelings. He thought he could hear a small song – was it in his mind? – was it in his ears? "Trust in me, trust in me, close your eyes, and trust in me...." His hand began to reach out to a blossom that suddenly seemed much closer than it had been before. He saw himself as a small honey bee delicately harvesting the nectar from this sweet flower. His arms and legs grew heavy as his spine lost its shape. There was something scaly and sinuous wrapped around one of the branches that called out to him with a soft, comforting voice. "Yesss, you can trussst the tree. Look at her glory, ssshe isss here for you. Ssshe will make you sssmarter; ssshe will help you understand the mysssteriesss of thisss place." Ray felt relaxed and calm. His brain was no longer a buzz of conflicting thoughts. He felt he could rest in this place for a while - just a while. His eyes closed and he was nearly asleep. Something brushed against his arm; a tiny flicker tickled his ear; something cold and scratchy touched his Adam's apple and disturbed his tranquility. He startled awake and looked around. Nothing but the tree and Sugar could be seen and he nearly went back to sleep despite the brightness of the day. One thought occurred to Ray as his mind began to blink on and off. He thought about long stretches of memory that had been lost to a bottle of gin. He wondered about this tree and its effects on his mind.

Ray turned to Sugar and asked him if he had thought about the long-term complications of such a diet. Was he not concerned about spending all his time in hallucinations and what that might do to his mind? Sugar said that he had thought about it but he could not bear to move away from Gloria. She brought him so much comfort. "Besides, I think I am getting more intelligent," he said. "If I stay here a little longer I think I might create something." Ray could feel his mind coming more alive as he asked more questions about Sugar's life. He asked Sugar if he wouldn't rather spend some time travelling to see other parts of this world. Sugar showed no interest even after Ray told him about some of the wonders he had already seen and how he expected to see more wonders over the next horizon. Ray was feeling stronger now. His arms, legs, and spine were regaining their strength and so Ray encouraged Sugar to travel along with him and even grabbed his arm to try and get him to join him on his trek. Sugar politely declined. "No, you go on ahead. What more could I want? I don't want to leave this place. I might not ever find my way back to this tree. I think I will just stay right here. Every day I take a trip and never leave the farm," he said with a smile. "Pass me those seeds, would you?"

Ray decided to move on without Sugar. The first few steps were a stumbling, comical display of mind over feet. The ground appeared close to Ray's face then swished away as if he might take flight. His next steps were more solid and his confidence increased with every step away from the tree. A low wind brought the sound of sliding scales and a soft hiss. He knew he was headed in the right direction. The wind rustled in the leaves of the trees and caused their scent to tangle with Ray's nose. The smell was sickeningly sweet in

Ray's nostrils and he never looked back as he moved on down the road.

7. Martha

The way became grassy and less treed. It was almost as if he were walking through fields of hay that were somewhat more wild than farmed land. The way opened into a deep valley with a river running along the bottom. Down the path a little further, for there was no road in this lush grassy land, Ray came upon a house decked out like he had never seen before. The roof and walls were covered in a dozen or more mechanical and electronic devices. There was a wind vane with a cupped wheel for measuring wind speed, a thermometer, a small observatory dome with telescope, a rain gauge, what looked like solar cells, a barometer, and several other apparatuses Ray could not identify. As he walked up to the front door he found it ajar and knocked and called out as he went in. Inside was an even larger array of instrumentation: microscopes, scales, centrifuges, water-baths, test-tubes, petri dishes, fume hoods, and once again several things he could not identify. Notebooks and laptops were scattered around the room, and a video camera seemed to be running in one corner of the room. Ray could see a woman with her back turned to him and she was staring at a large screen with waves of coloured lines flowing across it. She seemed engrossed in counting and held up one hand toward Ray as she counted and focused on the screen. She came to the end of a line and pressed a key that stopped the flow of waves across the screen and finally turned to look at Ray. The first words out of her mouth were, "Are you the student they sent over from the university? I was expecting someone considerably younger. Do you have any experience in genetics? That is what I really need right now. My own education is more in the field of engineering and geology, but I find right now that I need to do some genetic studies. I was hoping the university would send me a real whiz-bang kid to do the work."

Ray assured the woman that he had not been sent by the university and that he had no knowledge of genetics or engineering or geology. He told her he had simply been passing by on the road headed toward another destination when he saw her home. The woman introduced herself as Martha and asked where Ray was headed. Ray realized that he had no idea and stammered back some response about being on a quest to find the end of the road. Martha told him that her own quest was one of looking backward, trying to find the beginning of all roads. She had started in the field of geology and had studied the many layers of rock laid down in this part of the world showing the ancient nature of the planet. This had taken her into archeology as she had found more and more evidences of human civilization in her geological samples. Then, in turn, she studied fossils and tissues excavated from mines and deep places in the ground. Ray began to wonder just how long Martha had been working on her quest. She told him that right now she was trying to perfect her ability to do DNA sequencing. She was comparing the DNA of modern whales to that of an ancient and extinct dog-like creature that had lived in aquatic environments much like present-day otters. She had managed to get the equipment and taught herself how to use it, but she found it to be a significant amount of work. She was hoping to get some help. She wondered if Ray might like to stay and help with the work. "Would you like some tea?" Martha asked. "I am pretty sure we still have some somewhere around here. Let me boil some water." Martha lit a Bunsen burner under a large glass flask. Ray thought he recalled this type of flask being called an Erlenmeyer and realized that might be the extent of his knowledge of science.

Ray wanted to be polite and agreed to stay until they had some tea, but Martha got distracted looking for the tea and got engrossed in one of her lab notebooks. It did not seem like Ray was going to be drinking tea any time soon and so he began to look about in the many rooms of the house. Here was a whole room devoted to the morphology of animals. Martha had pictures of whales, dolphins, orca, and what must have been their pre-historic ancestors. She had a taxidermy collection of birds with variously shaped beaks. Another room was filled with rocks and geological samples. Still another room had large freezers and canisters of liquid nitrogen with tissue samples. Ray wondered where she got her supply of equipment and consumable materials. It wasn't like there was a scientific supply store around the corner. He realized it was just one more way this world into which he had fallen was unusual and had to be some sort of alternate reality.

Ray soon became bored looking at all the stuff Martha had in her house. He knew that he would not make a very good scientist; he just wasn't as curious as Martha. He knew he would have to get out of this house soon. He went back to see what Martha was doing. When he walked into the room she looked up from a microscope and for a second he thought she had forgotten his name or having seen him before. Then a faint recognition crossed her face and she told Ray to make himself useful and read the sequences that were spewing out of the sequencer. "You know I can't do all this work on my own," she said. Martha went back to her microscope and Ray took that opportunity to sneak back out the way he had come in. He felt sorry for running away like that, but he comforted himself knowing that Martha would forget about him in a day or two.

As he left Martha's place and began to climb out of the valley in which he had found her, darkness fell once again and Ray had to find a spot to rest. He nestled into a luxurious bed of grass and creeping vines that proved to be a more comfortable bed than any on which he had slept.

8. The Statues

The way was more open now and the lush grass of the valley gave way to scrub-brush and dry prairie grasses. Ray could see a forest on the horizon. There seemed to be no better direction to go and so he kept walking toward it. As he got closer, he could see trees at the edge of the forest and something else within the trees. He soon realized that there were only a few trees in this forest and the rest of the objects were statues. They appeared to be the most perfectly carved statues of people. Every detail and colour was perfect; it was as if each one had been molded from an animate person and then dressed in clothes. The next thing he noticed about the collection of statues was that they were all walking and headed in the same direction: the very direction Ray was headed. But, and here was what made the whole thing so eerie and odd, they were all looking over their shoulder behind them. They looked as if they could not quite decide which way to go, as if they were being drawn by the road behind. Ray looked closer and saw that the statues were interacting perfectly with their environment. They were not a group of statues that had been made somewhere else and then brought to this place. They were shaped as if they were walking around trees, stepping on stones crossing streams, tripping over roots in the ground. He touched one or two of the statues and found that they were incredibly dense and hard. He doubted that a knife would scratch the surface of any of them. They were also cold to the touch, so cold that they seemed to extract all the heat out of Ray's body and made him shiver. He soon stopped touching any of them. He was aware of a low quiet rumble that he could not identify. The frequency was down below the deepest of whale sounds. He could hear it despite it being very quiet.

Then he saw the most curious thing. He came upon a statue in mid-air. The statue was shaped in such a way that it appeared to have tripped over a rock and was falling through the air. The sculptor had caught every muscle perfectly and it was flying without apparent supports. The man depicted in the statue was slightly paunchy and the rolls of his stomach seemed to be pulled by gravity in a realistic way. Ray reached around the statue and swung his legs underneath to see if there were supports that were difficult to see. He could detect nothing. It was most curious and he wondered what he was missing. Right at that moment, darkness fell and Ray was once again left in blackness. He had been close enough to a tree that he could move just enough to snuggle up against the tree for some sleep. Compared to the statues, the tree felt remarkably soft and it seemed to Ray that it gave off a bit of warmth that restored his temperature after touching the figures.

Morning came and Ray felt refreshed from his sleep once more. He was again struck by the oddity of the field of statues. Where did they come from? Where were they all headed? Why were they looking back over their shoulders? It occurred to him that he should look over his shoulder and see what he could see but as soon as the thought crossed his mind it left him again and he did not look back. He began to look at some of his favourite statues from the day before. It was almost like living in an art gallery and Ray began to appreciate the aesthetics of his environment. He noticed how each statue looked different from other angles; he could almost believe that they were moving. It looked like their eyes had shifted in their heads and that their gaze was slightly different.

Then he saw something that stopped his thoughts and chilled his heart. The paunchy man was no longer in mid-air. One arm was thrust at a strange angle as if he had tried to catch himself and his right cheek was sunk into the gravel of the path. A bright red blotch could be seen expanding from the point of impact. Ray stood staring for a moment taking in what he was seeing. Had the sculptor returned in the night and replaced the statues with new ones? He could now see that there were many subtle changes in most of the figures around him. Certainly such activity would have woken him in the night. No, there had to be some other explanation. It seemed to Ray that the only plausible explanation was that these were not statues at all. Perhaps they were indeed animate people that were moving extremely slow, or was he moving extremely fast? Time seemed to be a difficult concept in this place. No two days were the same length and some days moved fast while others moved glacially slow. Could it be that time was moving at different speeds for him and the statue people? That would explain how they were hard and immovable, yet not quite static.

As he thought about these things he wondered why these people would be moving so slowly. It again occurred to him to look over his shoulder, but he quickly put it out of his mind. He pressed on through the crowd of statuesque people. Should he keep going forward or return on the path on which he had come? He stole a quick look over his shoulder. As he did, every statue became animated and he could see their movements and hear their voices. They were all walking forward and looking back and grumbling along the way. He heard things like, "I should have never started out on this journey. Who is leading us? Where are we going? I want to go back." Ray turned his eyes forward and everything returned to its previous state. Now he understood the low rumbling sound. It was all the conversations slowed down like an LP record played at a very slow speed. He was tempted to join them by looking over his shoulder again but he was afraid that if he did that he might never return and would be stuck with this grumbling horde of people forever. He resolutely looked forward and pressed on as quickly as he could through the crowd. The crowd of statues began to thin out until he came to a very few at the front edge of the group. Then he spotted one old man with a long walking stick at the very front of the crowd. The stick had an odd carving on the top of it; it looked like it had a snake wrapped around it. The old man was also looking over his shoulder as if he were urging those behind to keep on following. Ray was mesmerized by the snake. The walking stick was nothing special, even though it was rather tall for this grizzled old man, but the snake held Ray's attention in a way he would not have thought possible. Simply gazing at the snake made his heart feel lighter and his body sounder. After a few more minutes of looking at the snake, Ray moved on. A few more kilometers down the road, night returned and Ray slept a deep and dreamless sleep.

9. The Fort

He awoke in the morning feeling set for whatever this day might bring. Ray was beginning to wonder about his purpose in this place. How long could he journey in this strange Venusian landscape? He became aware that he had not once needed anything to eat in this world in which he now found himself, this world that had opened outside of his truck and the well-site field. What sort of place was this? He wondered how he might get out of this world.

As he came over the next rise, Ray saw a fort with a high wall of logs anchored in the ground as if planted by a giant hand. These posts were set tight to each other, lashed together with swatches of colourful cloth, and sharpened on top. The trailing bits of bright cloth gave the wall a festive look that suggested pavilions and flags. The wall surrounded a small house or perhaps a storage shed. Only the very top of the building was visible over the wall, but Ray could catch glimpses of the rest of it through tiny chinks in the surrounding fence. Despite the crude materials used to build the structures, there was an elegance and attention to detail that caught Ray's eye. The gate was closed and a small bell allowed visitors to announce their presence. Ray rang the bell and waited to see what would happen. The gate looked like it could be let down in the fashion of a drawbridge, and had a small door built into the middle of it to allow for the entry of one person at a time. The door had a 15-centimeter hinged opening in the middle that swung inward and it was there that a face soon appeared. The face, although once pretty, was twisted as if it had been damaged by an accident. The face was there for just an instant and then it was gone. A voice that sounded vaguely familiar said, "With a word, you can get what you came for." Recognizing the paraphrase of a song, Ray's automatic response was "gold." A laugh from within was the reply and the door swung open. The woman inside was dressed in a long flowing dress with puffy sleeves and a voluminous skirt. The dress touched the ground and made a swishing sound as she walked. The outer shell of the dress was a brilliant purple and shone with reflected sunlight. It looked noble and elegant and suggested another time and another place. The woman's hair was long, tangled, wild, and looked as if birds might make a nest in it. She kept her face turned mostly away from Ray and the long frizzy locks covered her profile.

She showed him around and told him how she had built this place herself. In the early days, she had plied her abilities as a seamstress as she made clothing and fancy costumes, which she then traded for gold. She had catered to a lot of performers and musicians. They were the best customers; no outfit was too extravagant and no price too high. Yet such customers could be demanding and they sometimes wanted more than she could give. She had found ways to protect herself from those who wanted too much. As she acquired more wealth, she had used some of her gold to buy the logs and other things she needed. Most of the fortifications had risen straight out of her mind. Ray wondered what she meant by this but thought that it was a creative way of describing how things were built in this place.

Ray asked the woman by what name he should call her. She laughed and said that her name was Magill, and she called herself Lil, but everyone knew her as Nancy. Ray could tell that there was more to this enigmatic, lyrical answer but decided not to push it. He smiled and said that, in that case, she could call him Rocky Racoon. There was something sad and broken in "Magill" and keeping her name from him was one more defensive mechanism. What was it that was so familiar about this woman? Why, of all the people he had come upon, did she seem to draw him? Was that a faint scent of a familiar perfume on the wind? He wished he could see her better; he wished her hair would fall back and reveal her face; he wished he could remember what he had seen in the moment her face had been visible in the gate. Had she recognized him? Was that what that faint light in her eyes had been?

There was a certain familiar easiness with which they talked. She spoke of being in this place for years and how at first, she had thought it was some alternate reality in which she might be able to ask all her questions and find answers. But she soon realized that there were no more answers here than there had been anywhere else. It was one more place of disappointment. She had found no more love here than she had in other places she had lived.

As a young and beautiful girl, she had high hopes of finding a man who would love her deeply. She had used her beauty and charm to catch the eye of high-school quarterbacks and rock stars before turning to businessmen and those who allowed her to dress in lace and go places in their expensive cars and make entrances in style. But she seemed to have a weakness for finding men who liked to use their fists and the fairy-tale romances always lost their bloom. By the time she made it to this place, she was wary, protective, and less beautiful than she had once been. She had cried out to God and asked him to restore her beauty, but God was silent. She cried out for love, but God was silent. She had asked for a new name and a new face, but God was silent. After that she had simply settled here. She had settled for this life, this existence, this place where she could be safe and live how she wanted to live. No one could touch her, no one would push her around. She was a rock, and an island. She felt no pain and cried no tears. This would be her motto and this would be her flag. But there were times when she would let someone through the gate.

Night began to fall and small lights came on around the inside of the fort giving the courtyard the look of a European side-street. Ray had not noticed cobblestones beneath his feet, but there they were now. He could hear cicadas and somewhere a single violin was playing. The sky above was lit with the grandeur of millions of stars. Previously he had not seen a single star as he travelled this planet and so it surprised him to see them now. They reminded him of home and he felt that he might warm up to this part of the planet. There was something enticing about this place, this woman, and this moment. Everything felt different now. He turned in time to see the woman's hair go from wild and tangled to smooth, silky, and beautiful. She shook it away from her face and their eyes met for the first time. She saw him, knew him... and hated him. He saw her, knew her, and his heart went cold. He had not recognized her before. There was some trick of this place that made everything look normal and plain and everyday. But nighttime revealed the truth.

Ray knew in an instant that he must leave! He stumbled toward the gate, rattled the latch until it released, pulled the door toward him and staggered out into the night. The night was much darker outside the fence and his legs seemed intent on tripping him up. He sprawled in the sand outside the fort just beyond the reach of light and sound. The drawbridge came down with a crash, narrowly missing his feet. The woman in all her terror stood at the end of the giant bridge towering over Ray. She seemed to scream his name but no sound came out. Her form turned ghostly and a breeze tore through her as if she were made of smoke. Ray heard the drawbridge creaking back into place as all around him went black.

He could not tell how long he lay in terror and utter blackness. When he finally rose in the light of another day, there was no evidence of the previous events. The fort was gone and a road stretched out before him inviting him to carry on. He could almost believe the events of the day and night before were all a dream... almost. He dusted the dirt off his pants and shook a tangle of red hair from his shoulder. Ray walked on. For what seemed an eternity, his mind was frozen. When he would try to make sense of things he could not focus. He would find himself thinking of a beautiful fort and a courtyard, but his brain could not advance to the next moments of the story. His heart was frozen in time and his thoughts became cyclical as he ruminated over and over about the exact same things. A sense of self-loathing was the only clear emotion.

10. The Tree

Lost in his thoughts, Ray came upon the largest tree he had ever seen. He thought that it must be the largest tree in all of history. He first saw it from a half kilometer away. The trunk of the tree was massive and it had many leafy branches. Where it disappeared above him in the clouds, the trunk was still massive and appeared to reach far up into the sky. Ray paused on a hill close to the tree and watched for a while. He watched as others made their way to the base of the tree. He could hear snippets of conversation as people gathered around the base and as they walked past him. Sitting there for hours, Ray could piece together what was going on and what the tree represented. This was a proverbial magic beanstalk. People were coming from all around and many had searched for a long time to find this tree. They believed that if they climbed this tree they could escape endless walking on the Venusian soil and arrive in a new place, a Nirvana of rest and peace and luxury. Some of the people spoke of streets paved with gold and rivers that flowed with wine. No one was ever sick and life was a constant joy in the land at the top of the tree. The tree had been planted many years ago by a group of people who believed that one day this tree would rescue them from Venus. They tended it carefully, providing just the right nutrients and water in the hope that the tree would be tall enough to get them out of this land.

There were also stories that the first Tenders of the Tree, for that is what they were known as, had been so consumed by the job of caring for the tree that they had ceased to exist. The people of Venus had installed others in the office of Tenders of the Tree and had set appropriate boundaries in place. The new Tenders of the Tree were only on duty one hour a day and spent the rest of their time praying for the growth of the tree. Tenders of the Tree knew that they could never join the others in climbing the tree and finding their way to the land above the clouds but sacrificially gave of their lives so that others might climb the tree and see the world above.

But Ray was not sure that all was as it seemed with the tree. True, people were climbing the tree and not coming back down. But there were signs that there may have been some distress. The higher they climbed the harder the climbing seemed to be. The tree proved to get more sticky as one climbed higher. When the clouds cleared for moments at the higher levels, Ray thought he saw people struggling in the branches. He thought he heard screams. At one point, he was almost sure he saw a face in the bark of the trunk. It looked like the person's face was frozen in terror and that perhaps their whole body had been absorbed by the tree. What if the tree was somehow luring people to climb it for its own benefit? What if people were the food of the tree? Was Ray witnessing some sort of bizarre Venus flytrap plant? A giant "Little Shop of Horrors" plant? This seemed too strange and too dangerous to Ray. He vowed he would not climb the tree, and yet he still felt the draw. He still wanted to climb the tree and get away from this land and ascend to some other place. The desire to be someplace else was now undeniable. He truly wanted to go somewhere other than here, anywhere other than here. Perhaps he should just climb the tree and get it over with. Being inside a tree was being somewhere else.

Ray got down from the little hill and moved steadily toward the tree. He could see the people clamouring over each other, trying to be the next to climb the trunk. Ray was drawn, and he moved closer. He could feel the tension of wanting to climb and wanting to run far, far away. He moved closer. He could now feel the tree calling to him. He could sense the stickiness of the bark. He wanted to touch it himself and push his hand into the softness of the tree. He wanted to pull on the branches and let them entangle him in their grasp. He wanted to be smothered in the leaves. At the last possible second his mind became clear for just a moment. He pulled away from his thoughts and ran as fast as he could down the path beyond the tree. Ray had escaped the power of the tree.

But no sooner had he done this than Ray began to think of others who were in danger of the tree. He turned and bolted back to the tree. He saw a young man just about to launch himself up the tree. He called to him and told him to stop but he was already far up the tree. He thought he heard a low growl emanating from the tree but then he thought, "No, that can't be." He set his sights on saving another person. A middle-aged woman had just begun to find some foot and hand-holds on the tree. Surely he could rescue her. Ray spoke with the woman and coaxed her down from the tree. He explained his concern about the nature of the tree. She listened for a moment but then went right back to climbing the tree. Ray grabbed her arm and interfered with her reach. He could feel the tree sticking to her hand as he pulled it away. Now he felt certain that there was a deep malevolence proceeding from the tree toward him. The woman had wrenched her arm away from him and was looking at Ray as if he was a threat. She kicked him in the jaw as she found a grip on a limb above his head. The branch swooped up as if moved by a strong wind – but there was no wind. The woman's feet were now securely stuck in the bark of the tree and the bark seemed to be moving on the trunk of the tree. When Ray could next focus, the tree had absorbed her legs up to the knees and the woman was oblivious to the consuming nature of the tree. The last Ray saw of the woman was a look of surprise when her breathing became difficult. Her body was now engulfed up to her chest and she finally felt the pressure. It was too late; all Ray could do was look on in horror. The light began to fade from the woman's eyes.

Ray looked down in time to see a small root wrapping itself around his ankle. He jumped free and ran quickly away from the tree. This time he heard a haunting and hideous laugh coming from the base of the tree followed by a whimper that sounded like the tree pleading with him to come and join it. Ray moved on.

11. Choices

But now, the die had been truly cast. Ray knew that he wanted to leave this planet. He was through with seeing the sights of Venus. He was through with seeing the many attempts of people seeking happiness in this place. He was through with the traps and dangers of this place. But how could he leave? He asked the question aloud: "How do I leave this place? God, help me! How do I get away from here?" No sooner had he said the words than his feet began to get light. At first he could not get traction on the road. He was slipping and not gaining ground. Then a small amount of space began to open between his feet and the road. He pushed and stretched his legs and toes, but the gap only widened. Next, he began to feel his body slowly rotate. His feet were making their way toward the sky again. When his feet were mostly pointed toward high noon, he began to feel himself falling again. Again, he was falling upward through the sky. As the nauseated feeling in his stomach returned, Ray began to have second thoughts. "Um, God, or whoever it is that caused this – I am not so sure about this falling!"

Shreds of clouds began to go by, slowly at first but soon very fast. Ray's stomach churned and did loops but there was no stopping the process. What had been started by his vocal cries could not be undone. He was falling out of the grip of Venus. Many of the colours he had seen on his entry into this world became evident once more as he retraced his journey up through the layers of atmosphere. Soon Ray could make out one or two stars, then a few more, and finally his whole view was nothing but stars and the bright glow of Venus behind him. After such a long time on the cloud enshrouded surface of the planet without, for the most part, seeing stars to guide him, the immensity of space unsettled Ray. He felt as though he might get sick. He felt as if he might crash into the piercing white of one of the stars. He felt as if he might drown in the enormity of black space. He knew he was quoting something from his past, but spoke it aloud anyway, as he hoarsely croaked, "My God, it's full of stars."

So began the next part of Ray's journey. He could not tell if it lasted hours or years. His mind was racing, his body ached one moment, and swam in comfort the next; sometimes this occurred at one and the same time. He found that he once again had control over his movement and could determine which direction he travelled. For a long time, he stayed in the shadow of Venus. He knew that the sun was somewhere behind that greenish glowing ball. For some reason, he found himself wanting to stay in the radiance and protective shadow of Venus. He even slowed his departure from the vicinity of the planet enough to avoid seeing the sun until finally it could no longer be avoided.

The sun rose with a sharp brilliance that Ray thought might tear flesh from his bones. There was no way he could look toward it. His eyes would have melted in their sockets. Then he did turn just enough to see the most brilliant colours he had ever seen. Colours such as this did not exist in the world in which he had been born. He thought that someone must have invented a new spectrum since he had spent time in school. He was immediately flooded with a sense of joy, peace, and well-being. He thought of all the differences he had seen in his life. He thought of all the colours of people he had known and how he had not trusted people of other colours and other cultures. Compared with the colours he now saw, the skin colours, the tree colours, the colours of animals and butterflies of his past, all looked like different shades of grey.

The hues of this sunrise quickly faded and Ray was left alone to his thoughts in a world of dark space and bright stars. Again, choices had to be made. Which way should he go? Toward the sun? Away into darkness? Toward a star? Ray knew the answer. He did not know why, but he knew that he was supposed to travel toward the sun. For what felt like three days, he went a different direction, not anywhere specific, just away from the sun. For about a week, he travelled toward the brightest star in what used to be his southern skies. He thought he remembered the star being called Sirius. He could now see that he was gaining ground on this star. It was getting closer. How fast must he be travelling now? Sirius began to look the size of the full moon viewed from earth. He could just make out some planets circling around the star. They were zooming around like bees at a hive and had their own intrinsic colours. He thought how it might be nice to settle down on one of these planets. He could be the king of his own space, perhaps even a god. He set his eyes on one of the rapidly moving spheres. He began to call it Sirius One. It looked like a nice little place, plenty of clouds, plenty of water, plenty of sun, and plenty of trees. It looked ripe for a coup. He would sweep in with all his might and speed while the entire planet was unaware. He would choose a high mount and set a large throne on top of a large city. The animals, plants, and people of that place would serve his needs. Perhaps he might even find a consort suitable to his needs. She would have to be strong and beautiful to inspire the worship of her people. He was sure that he would eventually find the right woman. He thought of Matthew Sunday and the paradise he had created for himself. Suddenly he was filled with loathing and realized what he was thinking about. He thought about the cage that Matthew Sunday had created, a cage for Matthew and a prison for the women who loved him and loathed him at the same time.

Suddenly the little planet next to Sirius did not look so appealing. He pushed hard and did his best to put on the brakes. He slipped through the atmosphere of Sirius One, bounced off a small moon, briefly riding in its gravity before finding himself in a tight orbit around the star itself. The maneuvers must have taken a week and he settled into a new routine around the star for the next month. By routine, he meant a routine of switching his gaze between three points: a gaze toward a faraway star that he knew to be his own home sun, a gaze toward the planet known to him as Sirius One, and a gaze toward the star called Sirius. Should he travel toward Earth's sun, stay near this sun called Sirius, or become a god on Sirius One? As his gaze wavered, so too did his mind. To which place should he go next?

The one thing he had come to learn about his new existence was that there seemed always to be another decision to be made. Each choice added a myriad of other choices, while also building a new set of rules and selection of choices. He wondered if his earlier life had been like this and he had not taken the time to notice the choices that were there. From the perspective he could see now, it appeared that in all his life he had been choosing the path of least resistance – ever going further down and further away from the ones he loved. Where had he gone wrong? What should he choose now? The easiest thing seemed to be the places that were closest to him. It would be so simple to fall into a star or take over a planet. The hard choice would be making his way all the way back to the sun. What was the right choice? What was the proper decision? His heart knew what was right. Could he make his mind believe it?

He thought about the path of least resistance he had taken in what had been his life before this place; Caroline, the cute girl in the bar who was ready to have some fun; the path of non-committal pleasure that had led to the pregnancy; the days when he chose the bottle rather than working things out with Caroline. He thought about the years of going to work and coming home, living from paycheque to paycheque, not rocking the boat, not really living life. He thought about the ways he had raised his son and the ways he had helped Ray, Jr. choose the easy path. He thought about his granddaughter, Evelyn, and how he had not done anything to make himself more fit to be a grandfather. He had never once prepared himself to be a father, a father-in-law, a grandfather, a husband.... He had never thought to pick up a book and read anything that might have made him a better man, a better father.... Why had he wasted all those years? What could he do now?

The drift continued for what must have been days. Each time Ray thought he would make up his mind, something else occurred to him. What if he could take care of the creatures on Sirius One? What if the people there needed him? What if there were no people on the planet and the planet itself needed him to care for its needs? Sometimes the distraction was simply a pretty flash of light from a distant star or planet. The ellipse around the star continued for several more revolutions.

A supernova flashed brilliantly in a far distant galaxy and Ray contemplated the universe in which he found himself. Was this universe just a product of chance or could it be that there was a creator, a prime mover, a first cause? Suddenly he knew the path he must take. It was not the easy path. It was not the path toward being the god of a planet. It was not the path of revolving endlessly around a small star. Immediately, his body was ejected out of orbit and sent directly toward that tiny sun far off in the distance. He headed toward that sun that he now knew as home.

The journey, though it was extremely long, took almost no time at all. Ray remembered feeling the buffeting of the edges of solar systems and the relative peace of the vast inter-solar spaces. He had a brief glimpse of a large planet which he knew had to be Saturn. He wished there was more time to explore its beautiful rings. Next he saw the giant red spot on Jupiter and again wished for a chance to look around. Mars, Earth, and Venus whipped by in rapid succession. Mercury went by a little slower and soon Ray found himself in a tight orbit around the sun. The light and heat should have been too intense for him, but somehow his eyes and his skin were protected from the punishing radiation. Time slowed again as his body got used to revolutions around this familiar sun and Ray wondered what would happen next. Each "year" of revolution in this place took only minutes but seemed like a month. Suddenly he was falling again. The drop onto Venus had not destroyed him but now he could see no possible way for his body to survive a plunge into the intense heat of a star. He could not precisely remember the surface temperature of the sun, but he knew it had to be several thousand degrees Celsius. Flesh could not survive such heat. He was aware of all of this as relentlessly his body dove deeper toward the surface of the sun.

He was not sure when it happened, but there was a change as he came close to the surface of the sun. At some point, his body simply vaporised. Ray was aware that he had become a wispy ghostlike being and the surface of the sun, which should have been molten liquid or gaseous, felt hard like packed clay. He found himself walking on the surface of the sun, if a wispy vapour of a ghost could be said to be walking. He was aware that there would be no more night in this place. The sun was not above, as he had always known it to be. It was now below his feet. There were no shadows, no shade, nothing cool, no water, and no sleep. None of these could exist in this place. But there was a road. So the vapour that had once been his body made its way along the road to see what he might see.

12. Siddhartha

He lamented the loss of his body. His shoes were now transparent bits of stuff that could not even be called molecules. He could see his toes through those shoes, but at the same time he could see the road through his toes. He no longer had a paunchy beer belly. Technically, he had no belly, no skin, no intestines, no spine, and no face. Yet there was a wispy remnant of all those things present. He looked at the place where his left arm should be, and saw a willowy thread of something. There was even some representation of the wedding ring that he still wore. He felt sad that he would never have his solid body again. Where were the scars he had received as a child when he played Evil Knievel on his bicycle? Where was that burned patch of skin on his right arm where he had tangled with a live electrical wire just last week? He missed those things. On the other hand, his hips and knees that always felt stiff and a little painful felt marvellous now. There was no evidence of the diabetes that had been a constant companion for over ten years. Was this Heaven? Was this Hell? Perhaps this was Purgatory. How could he tell? Was it a good thing or a bad thing that he no longer had a body? His mind wandered through these thoughts as he wandered down the road.

Ray tried to figure out where each part of his body used to be. Was there a face above his misty shoulders? Could anyone see his face? Did he have a stubbly beard on that face? He tried creating different expressions: a smile, a frown, a wink. Was he having any effect? Did he even have a face? What kind of face might others have in this place? He began to think of his old face as a mask he had worn. It seemed to Ray that he had now found a truer face and might yet find his truest face.

His thoughts grew more philosophic and he found himself thinking about the concept of God. Did God have a face? Surely, God must have a face. If anyone or anything had a face, surely God must have the truest face of all. There could be no mask upon the face of God. Yet Ray wondered about the many gods he had encountered in the worlds before this one. It seemed there had indeed been masks that represented God, a whole totem-pole filled with the masks of God. Which God, which gods, which face, was the face of God? He was suddenly overwhelmed by such thoughts and he could think on these things no more.

There were hills in the road and as he came up over a rise he came upon a building with wide eaves and five steps leading to a large door. On one side of the door stood a gong hanging from two chains in a wooden frame with a mallet hanging on one side of the frame. Ray thought about ringing the gong and seeing who might be summoned, but in his present ghostly condition, he felt it unlikely that he could lift the mallet. He silently made his way indoors. A lone man sat in the building. He was seated on a low cushion staring toward the door and saw Ray as soon as he came in. Perhaps Ray was not as transparent as he thought. Even inside a building like this the light and heat were intense. The building appeared to be made of granite or other hard stone, but despite this, the sun shone through the floors, the walls, the ceiling and everything in the room with very little diminishment. This gave everything a transparent and spectral appearance.

"Welcome home, traveller," said the man. "I am Siddhartha. After your long journey, you have reached your destination. Welcome to Nirvana." With these and other words, Ray's new companion began to tell him of this place he had come upon. Siddhartha praised Ray for his persistence in finding his way to this place. Sid (as he liked to be called by the younger novices) spoke to Ray of his own long journey through many cycles of life, many ups and downs of joy, despair, and self-denial. Siddhartha told Ray that he had built this place with his own mind and had been living here for years welcoming more and more people to join him in paradise. Ray wondered where all the others might be. It seemed that Siddhartha was the only one around. When Ray asked about this, he was told that a great many people had been through the temple but none had yet chosen to stay. Most stayed for a while and told Sid how much they loved the temple; they spoke of the peace that they felt in this place; then they would move on down the road. Siddhartha was convinced that it was because they had not yet renounced some of their cravings and attachments to the world. He assured Ray that these others would be back when they realized the error of their ways. He was certain that eventually all would see that this was the end of the journey.

Ray did think that Siddhartha's life was peaceful, but how long could one stay here in one place focused on blank walls? Sid encouraged Ray to join him in allowing the quiet emptiness of the temple to fill every corner of his mind. When Ray asked questions, Sid would tell him to empty his thoughts of the questions he might have, and fill his mind with the peace of the temple. Siddhartha had seemed friendly and inviting at first, but as the days wore on, he became more and more quiet. When Ray would begin to ask a question, Sid would tell him that this was the place where all questions had ceased. This was the end of the journey. This was the emptiness they had long looked for. They could now enjoy the quiet, the emptiness, the nothingness of being. One day when Sid seemed particularly absorbed in meditating upon the smooth surface of one of the transparent walls, Ray moved on.

13. Pilgrimmage

The void of his mind was immediately filled with Lydia. Her beautiful red curls, her perfume that reminded him of Scottish thistles in summer, her amazing smile, filled every corner of his frail being. Ray and Lydia had dated, even while Ray lived with Caroline. They had kept it a secret then. She lived with her mother and so their moments together were mostly spent as friends. Yes, they had slept together three times in their life, but this was not the focus of their relationship. Sex had made things more complicated, so they preferred to stay "just friends." They "got each other," and they loved nothing more than spending an evening together playing cribbage and talking music. Caroline was not a music buff and as much as Ray had tried to engage her in such conversations, he could not raise her interest above a simplistic level. Ray and Lydia, on the other hand, could quite literally go on and on about music for hours. Obscure lyrics were a favourite pastime. No band or type of music was off limits: country, pop, movie soundtracks, stage musicals, Led Zeppelin, Simon and Garfunkel, The Beatles, Eric Church, Tim McGraw, The Bee Gees, Leo Sayer, Elton John, Alan Parsons Project, Jon Foreman, Katy Perry, Lady Gaga, The Eagles, Wayne Kirkpatrick, Garth

Brooks, even Chris Gaines. Oh, the fun they had trying to stump each other!

Ray felt the old melancholy coming back to him. The relationship had been so sweet and so beautiful; until he broke it. He tried to slap himself in the face in disgust over what he had done, but his willowy arm passed through his flimsy face and he felt nothing. He put these things out of his mind and concentrated on the road he could see through his feet.

Almost instantly, Ray found himself running on a well-worn path with hundreds or possibly thousands of people dressed from head to foot in white cloth. Not an ankle or wrist showed. The crowd was jogging along with him through the undulating surface of the star, which now took the form of sand dunes. Ray felt that he had become less vaporous and slightly more solid, as if his body was getting used to the gravity and light of this place. Ray could not immediately tell who these people were. They seemed to be from several people groups: European, Asian, British, and Canadian. The crowd was working hard at running toward a place that he could not yet determine, but he knew there was a destination in the mind of each runner. The throng of people began to swing gradually left, and as they did, Ray was pulled along with them. It made him think of black starlings in tight formation, swarming through the skies, and changing direction without a signal. He was now sure that the crowd was made up of hundreds of thousands of persons.

A horn sounded and the entire crowd raised their hands to the sky and shouted, before dropping to the ground as one. With heads pointed in the direction they had been running, hands spread on the sand, and foreheads on the ground, every person spoke almost the same words. Ray could not make out what was being said but he felt certain that it was a prayer. As quickly as they had stopped, the crowd was up and running again. Now it seemed that the direction of motion was moving toward some point that could not yet be seen. The crowd of people stretched as far as Ray's eyes could see. He was just aware of a small dot in the centre of the crowd. It now looked like a black cube and Ray tried to work out what it was he was seeing. The cube was at the centre of a large coliseum with a counter-clockwise spiral of paths that led from the large dice-like object. He realized that all these people were on a pilgrimage to the cube.

Pulled by the crowd, from which he could not extricate himself, Ray moved with the throng to the large black block of rock. Each pilgrim before him would touch and kiss the block, shout something unintelligible to Ray, and then proceed to circle the rock seven times in a counter-clockwise motion. Not wanting to offend, Ray imitated the rest as best he could. He even made a little shout that sounded like what they were shouting. The sweat, the heat, the spinning of people, and the ecstasy of the crowd was beginning to wear upon Ray. He could feel a slow nausea rising in his throat. He wondered where he should throw up in this extremely crowded space and decided the best place to do this would be on his own shoes; his body obliged. He sprayed only a little on anyone else, and they did not seem to notice.

Eventually the crowd began to slow down and thin out. Where the others went, Ray could not tell, but go they did. Soon it was down to a small group of people jogging alongside Ray. He leapt out of the remaining group and threw himself panting on the ground. He found himself staring down at the sun and realizing that he was back to some semblance of a normal body with weight, and height, and solid bones. He could not be sure when this had happened but he was now sure that he was undeniably substantial once again. The remaining dregs of the crowd passed by Ray as he lay there in the road wondering what next would come upon him.

14. Companions

As he lay in the road, spent and exhausted, thoughts of his old life returned. He thought again of Lydia. Why had that relationship ended? It seemed he had put it so far out of his mind that he could barely retrieve the circumstances of the last time he had seen her. He tried to collect his thoughts and think back to that time. What had happened?

That portion of his mind seemed intentionally closed to him. He tried to reach back through the years to a time he could remember. Something was beginning to come clear. He could think of going by the Wicklow at the end of one of Lydia's shifts. She was in a happy mood because a wealthy regular at the bar had been flirting with her. She said it made her feel a little more alive. It made Ray feel jealous. Still, they had driven over to Ray's place and had been in good spirits as they sat down on the couch and turned on the TV to watch one of their favourite series on Netflix.

Again things got foggy and unclear in Ray's mind. He had an image of Lydia looking so beautiful sitting there on the couch. Her v-neck was slipping down just a bit and revealing more than Lydia normally let show. Ray reached over to give her a little kiss but Lydia quickly moved away and got up off the couch. Ray knew there had been some bad men in her life who had taken advantage of her in the past so he knew better than to press his luck with her, but something inside of him did not want to let it go this time. He asked why she had been so friendly with the customer at the bar but didn't have any time for him.

Again, mist, lost memories, things unclear. Ray could see things like he was looking through a foggy mirror. There must have been a big argument. Lydia pushed him and Ray gave her a small push back. Lydia had learned how to use her fists against men who tried to hurt her. He remembered a bruise or two he must have got from her. He tried to grab her wrists and keep her from hitting him. This had unleashed a blind fury in Lydia. Suddenly the fog cleared and Ray could see it all in a blinding sear of white light. He saw his arms reaching out to push her away so her fists couldn't reach him; her body falling; the side of her head connecting with the corner of a cupboard; her neck at an awkward angle. He ran to Lydia, weeping and immediately remorseful at what he had done. Why had she hit him so hard? Why had she pushed him? Why had he pushed her so hard? Oh Lydia, why, why?

From there, Ray had panicked. He picked up Lydia's lifeless body and propped her up in her car. He drove her out to the old quarry, about 5 kilometers out of town. He had some vague notion of making it look like a suicide. He propped her up in the car in the driver's seat and wedged her leg against the gas pedal. Ray left the motor running and dropped it into drive. The car had lurched and roared toward the big cliff. He watched it sail into the air and land with a terrible crash at the bottom of the quarry. He had hoped for an explosion, but with his rational mind he knew that only happened in the movies.

From there he just ran. As fast as he could he picked up his truck from Lydia's and drove. He spent a couple of days just driving and sleeping in his truck, thinking about next steps. When it seemed like people had accepted that Lydia had taken her own life, he went back to town and carried on with his normal life. He realized that it was only in the movies that the police investigated every detail so that no one ever got away. That was five years ago now.

Over time the guilt had gotten easier to handle. He told himself it was just an accident. He knew it was. People die in their homes every day. He loved Lydia. He hadn't meant to hurt her. Trudging through this alternate landscape, he could focus his mind on other things and keep the guilt at bay. But right now, in this place, something was gnawing at the edge of his brain. Something he had experienced in this place was beginning to make itself known and was intersecting with the world he had known before. He had almost put the fort incident out of his mind. Now it came flooding back: the woman, the recognition, her ghostly intensity, her eyes that bore through his very being. She... she was... she must be... her musical voice... her knowledge... the "password" that got him into the fort... the perfume on the wind... the romantic feel of the courtyard... the anguish... the hatred she had for Ray.

He realized how horrific it all was. He saw what he had done in a whole new way. He saw it through another's eyes. He knew he deserved to burn in hell. He screamed out to God, welcoming his own demise. He lay down and wept; he sobbed; he bawled; he shouted; but nothing happened. He lay in the road and nothing happened. He screamed at God again. He screamed at himself. He cursed the day he was born. His throat grew raw; his eyes could no longer weep. He lay in a puddle of his own blame wishing he could die. Nothing happened.

Eventually Ray got up and wiped his face. It seemed there was no God who would smite him today. He decided there was nothing to do but move on down the road. He walked for a long time lost in his thoughts, wondering when this nightmare would ever end. Why was he here? How did he ever get to such a strange place?

He saw another road joining the one on which he travelled and coming from this road were four people dressed in what could only be called Robin Hood clothing. Their hats each had a red feather sticking behind like the tail-feather of a rooster. Their legs were covered in dark coloured tights and from shoulder to mid-thigh they wore a green tunic. "Come and join us," the first one said. When Ray tried to protest, and tell them what he wasn't very good company and how tired he was, they all looked slightly suspicious and very concerned; another of them pulled out a vial of what looked like oil and made an X on Ray's forehead. Ray could barely believe what was happening, but after all he had seen and experienced, he wondered why this was so hard to understand. He immediately felt rejuvenated and about ten years younger. He also wanted to join the four, whatever quest they were on. They said that they were off to find the Fountain of Life, a stream that flowed out of a crystal bowl and sourced by an artesian spring. Ray thought, "Why not?" and got up and started walking. As they walked, the companions told him more about the fountain. It was very ancient and had been lost from all the maps of the world; only those of pure heart could now have any hope of finding it. Ray told the men that he was certainly not pure of heart. They told him he could start fresh today and encouraged him to come along on the journey.

They did not go far before they met a man dressed just like the others, standing on a stage with a curtain behind him, and shouting at the five of them. "Hello, step right this way, get your authentic 3-D map to the Fountain of Life. Simply lay down five payments of $25 each and the map will be yours. In no time, you too will be bathing in the Crystal Bowl as I have done myself. Step this way, don't miss out. This is a limited-time offer, so act now. There are just a few maps left. Enter into the most arduous, exciting, life-changing experience of your life. Change the world, by changing you!"

The man making all the noise certainly seemed in good health. His blonde hair reflected light like nothing Ray had ever seen before. Despite his apparent age, he had very few wrinkles, and his voice, although loud, had a soothing quality that made one trust him implicitly. As he made his pitch he told jokes, recounted stories from his life and generally made an appeal to the good will of all who heard him. Ray began thinking about the wallet he must have had when he started this journey and wondered if it had survived all his adventures. It certainly would be good to finally have a map of this curious world in which he found himself. But Ray's travelling companions warned him away from the man. They had gone to him before and found his maps to be lacking. They told him that they knew the way and the services of the Holy Man (as he was called) would not be needed. They told him he was just another hired-hand, a wanna-be prophet who made money off people's hopes and dreams. He promised peace, joy, health, and a happy life that he could not deliver. Ray had known others like the man they were now describing so he quickly moved away.

What was it about these preachers of truth that made them so believable? His mind went back to a trip to Houston, Texas, to a man who had promised a new and dynamic life. The sales pitch had been subtle at first. He remembered the music of the church service. It was loud and then soft, earnest, then unassuming, traditional, and then contemporary, jazz-infused and then bluesy; there was even a segment of street poetry from a young black man who had walked away from a life of drugs and loose living. Finally, when the crowd had experienced sufficient joy, angst, encouragement, and warning, the preacher walked on stage. His perfectly white smile seemed to light up the stadium-sized auditorium. His eyes sparkled with the reflected stage lighting. The words of the preacher's message followed the progression Ray had just witnessed in the music: soft and warm, slow and thoughtful, loud and energetic, earnest and entreating. He warned of impending doom and spoke of the safety in the shelter of his church. He spoke of false prophets who were trying to disrupt the work of this beautiful and hard-working group of people. He warned of the temptations of the world and how many had lost their way because they turned to a different voice.

The preacher's eyes somehow grew even brighter than they had before. His smile gleamed like a cartoon caricature. A tear streamed down one cheek and was caught on the large screen projection system. He implored his audience to join him in this most difficult, glorious, wondrous, dangerous, and hope-filled cause. Together, there was nothing they couldn't do. Together, they would rewrite history. Together, they could heal the ills of the nation and the world. They would take their message to those who needed it most in America. They would take their message to the godless hordes of the Middle East. They would win back these countries for the sake of those whom God had placed there first. They would be the remnant who followed God to the promised land.

As Ray reminisced about this experience he thought of how he had been caught up in the fever of that church in Texas. He had dropped a week of wages into the offering plate as it came by his seat. He had cried real tears for the way he had lived his life. He had cringed at the thought of being among the godless who suffered the wrath of God. He had walked out a changed man and promptly drank himself into a stupor in a blues bar on the lower east side.

15. The Fountain

As Ray and his companions continued their journey, the sand dunes gave way to low bushes, then small trees, and larger trees until they were in a lively forest with a myriad of birds, squirrels, rodents, rabbits, and creatures Ray had never seen before. There was a pig-sized creature that had armour plating like an aardvark but a head like a donkey. There was a monkey-like creature with a golden tail and a head that looked like a man's. It even looked like this creature might shave portions of its face and it wore a small loin-cloth at its waist. There was a tiny insect that looked like a military tank with one antenna in front and what looked like wheels and track where it connected with a leaf. Ray found himself wondering if he would ever get used to the surprises of this place. The assortment of plant life was equally varied. Ray had always thought that Earth was a diverse eco-system, but this place was truly beyond the scope of his home world. There were flowers the size of a mid-sized car, trees with bark that was pigmented and striped like a Siberian Tiger, and what must have been what the Beatles sang about in "Lucy in the Sky with Diamonds" - there they were, cellophane flowers of yellow and green towering over his head.

The land bordered on being swampy with many streams and pools winding through underbrush. Ray had tried to keep his feet dry for the first bit but soon realized that to be a hopeless cause. He sloshed through the ponds and creeks that were shallow and found his way around the waist-deep roaring rivers. At least getting his shoes wet had washed away the vomit from his last adventure.

His companions had a particular stream to which they were seeking to stay close. It was not the largest stream, but it bubbled along with a greater joy than any other in the region. The terrain was difficult and from time to time they had to stray away from the stream and lose sight of it. Ray could not be sure that they would then find the same stream again further up, but his colleagues assured him that they were still on track and were looking for the source of this brook. Occasionally they would reach down and cup a hand in the stream, taking a small drink to see how it tasted. Ray thought it tasted like any other stream: cool, refreshing, and slightly boggy like there must be peat moss somewhere upstream.

The journey was a long one. It seemed to go on for many days and perhaps even weeks, but in a place where there was neither sunset nor dark, it was especially hard to keep track of time. Over this period, Ray did not seem to need sleep. Was he getting energy directly from the sun? His companions never rested or slept. They doggedly followed the path, whatever that path was.

Eventually the five of them came to a gap in the trees. The grass was short, almost as if it had been mowed, but it was more ragged than mowing would have left it. Then he saw the reason. Several sheep seemed intent on keeping the grass at just a certain length. Ray could count five sheep within what must have been a hectare of land. But the most amazing thing about this patch of land was that about two meters into the area that was being trimmed by the sheep, rays of light and heat were rising 20 meters into the sky. It was as if the crust of the sun was broken in a perfect circle. It could have been a series of stovetop gas jets burning into the sky, but Ray thought it was something more natural than this. It was difficult to see through the rays; the brightness was even more intense than the light shining up from below his feet, but Ray could see something in the centre of the circle.

As his eyes adjusted to the new surroundings he could see that it was indeed a fountain. The bowl appeared to be made of marble and the central fount, from which large volumes of water gushed, was formed in the shape of a winged person with a sword. The water shot straight up in the air out of the end of the sword and landed directly in the large bowl beneath the fount. Where the water went from there was hard to discern at first. Then Ray noticed that on the far side of the fountain was a large crack in the bowl where water poured out and fed a stream that wound out of the glade and made its way through a tiny gap in the ring of fire. The stream that ran through the narrow gap bulged on one side such that much of the current flowed on the other side of the gap, while the side that swelled looked mostly still. Ray realized that it was through this gap in the ring that the sheep would come and go and he made his way through the opening sticking mostly to the side where the current was gentle. Two sheep looked up from where they drank at the edge of the quiet water. They did not seem the least bit frightened or concerned by his presence and went straight back to what they had been doing.

The four companions, who had been Ray's guides to this point in the journey, seemed suddenly hesitant. They had prepared for this moment and now they seemed cautious to move into this place for which they had searched. Ray found himself to be the curious one who wanted to explore the fountain that stood before him. He was drawn to the falling curtain of water in the bowl and he moved closer to it. The sound of the falling water as it struck the water in the bowl was mesmerising and intimidating. The sound seemed to be too harsh, as if the water were heavier than ordinary water. It sounded like it might crack Ray's bones if he dared to venture under the torrent.

Ray could hear his companions behind him now. They called out to him and told him to stop.

They said that he wasn't ready yet. They yelled that he was in danger. They suggested that they all just slow down and rest close to the fountain. They talked about building some shelters in which they could live right beside this glade. He could hear the bleating of sheep mixed with the sounds of their voices. He heard all of this but still his feet moved forward ever closer to the pummelling flood. He had come too far not to see this through to whatever the end might be. He felt like a man walking to his execution but strangely calmed by the force that drew him on.

He had reached the edge of the bowl; the sound of water was all he could hear. His leg lifted over the edge and he stood in water to his waist. Now he had to work hard to move forward toward the curtain of water. The water in the bowl was heavy and created much resistance against his body. It was thick like stew and he had to swing his hips to make progress through it. Oh, what would such heavy water do to him if he dared put his head beneath the flood? It would very likely crack his skull. Yet all he could think about doing was plunging his head into the roaring curtain. He broke through the curtain of cool crisp water with less effort than he had expected. The roar of the water was still deafening, but he had survived the force on every aspect of his being. He could not feel a single broken bone. He now stood in a ring of water that thrashed all around him, creating a relatively calm space at its core. It was like the calm place in the eye of a hurricane. He was thoroughly drenched and felt like a layer of his skin had been washed away. His skin and clothing felt refreshed, cleansed, and renewed. He thought all of this in just a moment as he realized that he must now press through the wall of water once again. As he passed through the water this time, the sound was that of a quick plunge in still water that ended with silence. He should have still been tremendously close to the roar of the water. Instead he found himself in a new world. The curtain of water had been a door into a silent new land.

16. The Man

Ray had watched plenty of science fiction movies about doors to new universes and new times, but this transition was different from them all. There was no light burst or stream of stars like those of a Star Trek movie. There was no spinning of the hands of a clock or image of falling endlessly through a tunnel. There was very little to indicate that any major transformation had occurred, and yet, Ray was certain that he had just travelled an enormous distance across an expanse of time. He was also sure that he was now far from the companions who had guided him to the fountain and he felt a small twinge of sadness at this realization.

The path went along for a while with only sparse vegetation; Ray soon found himself among the habitations of a small Middle-Eastern village. The sounds, smells, and feel of a town awoke old feelings of joy and he looked forward to interacting with the people of this place, yet somehow he couldn't quite engage the people. They seemed not to be able to see or hear him. There were signs in languages he could not read with crude pictures that suggested lodging and food. The places offered food and shelter for modest fees and were just now being opened for business by their proprietors. In all the time Ray had been in this alternate reality, he had not experienced hunger or thirst, nor had he needed shelter from the elements. As he wondered if he needed them now, he was aware of a small feeling of hunger that had just begun to make itself known.

Thinking about food and hunger caused Ray to think back through his experiences of the last while. Had he truly not been hungry, thirsty, cold, or in need of a place to sleep? His mind wandered back through all the experiences of his time beyond his everyday world and he wondered if he had seen all there was to see in this place. No, his mind was clear on that, he had not yet seen all there was to see. He also wondered if he should have stayed in one of the places through which he had passed. No, his mind was clear on that as well; he was on a mission to find something. What that something was, he did not yet know.

His mind flashed back to the truck, the well-site, and the remote place. How had he left that world? Was he supposed to leave that world? He thought perhaps he had been murdered. Could that be? Who would want him dead? He could not imagine who it would be. Had someone realized what he had done to poor Lydia? Had someone tracked him down and snuffed out his life? He wouldn't blame them if they had and again the old melancholy, sick feelings returned to his mind.

Ray thought back to the truck. He had a momentary image of spilled pills, and a bottle of whiskey at his feet in the cab of a truck. The momentary image changed to a more persistent picture of a mouthful of pills, choking and gagging, and a bitter taste in his mouth. He could feel nausea returning and his head felt like it had a Tilt-a-Whirl inside. He felt a stronger urge to put some food in his stomach and quell the sourness of his belly. Suddenly it all came clear. "My God, I murdered myself. God help me. What do I do now? Where am I? Am I destined to walk this road forever?" He sat on the side of the road weeping. All the evil, dark, hurtful things he had done came flooding back to him. The emotions of those he had hurt were clearly there in his mind. He wailed and sobbed and longed for release from these chains that had wrapped themselves around his throat.

A man appeared on the horizon. Despite his current state of mind, Ray saw the man and followed his movement toward him. He welcomed the distraction of looking at this person even as he knew that he had no desire to speak to the man. The man on the horizon drew closer and Ray could see that he looked like he was used to hard labour. His skin was exceptionally red like one who has worked long in the sun and is permanently stained by its rays. His shoulders were broad but he was not overly tall and he looked square with a low centre of gravity. His hands were the next thing to catch Ray's attention. They were bulbous, calloused, gnarly, and twisted as if they were used to hard use, but then had also been recently injured. Ray could see a number of scars and torn nails. The man's face was not exceptional, his ears were perhaps slightly large for the head but that may have been an illusion caused by the sheer redness of each one. His cheeks were hollow and the cheek bones showed a puffiness like that of a prize fighter. The nose had likely been broken and showed a prominent hump and a noticeable scar. If Ray had seen the man any other place, Ray would have most likely ignored the man. There was nothing about the man that attracted Ray to follow him with his gaze. Yet, in this present place and circumstance, Ray could not take his eyes off the man.

In fact, Ray could not take his eyes off this man's face. Ray had already concluded that it was not a handsome face. Quite the contrary, it looked rather asymmetric and coarse. It was the kind of face that made you think that this person had once been very sick. Had he suffered a stroke? The cheek on one side of the face sagged more than the other side. One eye was larger than the other and the colour of each iris was slightly different. The brow was wrinkled, and the smile lines around his eyes were prominent. One cheek looked hollow while the other was puffed up as if it had recently taken a blow.

There was something else to be noted about this face. Ray marvelled that the man's face seemed to be very open. That was the only way to explain it. There was not a trace of shyness, anger, dishonesty, or anxiety. Ray could well imagine that this face had never once deceived anyone; the man's emotions had never been concealed. He lived a life that allowed all to see him as he was. It slowly dawned on Ray that he was seeing a person who had no mask. The face that this person showed to the world was a perfect representation of the man's heart.

"Hello friend," Ray heard him say and wondered at this familiarity. They were certainly not friends. Ray had never seen the man in his life. Yet there was a familiarity about him. Ray felt that maybe he had met him before, but then he thought that this must be the commonness of the man. He looked like everyman and no man.

"May I walk with you a while?" asked the man, who did not offer a name. Ray did not want to ask the man his name but offered his own. The man said, "I know." He turned and joined Ray in his direction and Ray wondered if the man went back and forth often. Despite Ray's thoughts about the man and the openness of his face, Ray could not help but think, "What is his game? What does he want from me?" The short legs and plodding steps of the man slowed Ray's progress and he was just about to press on ahead when the man asked him what he had been thinking about when they had met. Ray's mind was suddenly overwhelmed with emotion and a flood of thoughts. Did this man suspect the shame that

Ray felt? No, that couldn't be. Ray worked his way around the question without answering.

They talked for a while like old friends do. The man was marvellous at conversation and Ray felt at ease despite the sudden waves of pain, shame, and remorse that coursed through him every few minutes. They spoke of Ray's son, granddaughter, and a son Ray did not know he had. He was not surprised to discover this son and did not think to ask the man how he knew about a person that was Ray's own son. Ray spoke of joy mixed with sorrow, mixed with regret, mixed with unfulfilled dreams. No stone was left unturned. At the end of many kilometers and many broken-hearted stories, Ray looked up to see that they had walked through almost all of the village, or was it a city? The place must have been bigger than he had imagined.

Now Ray was famished. All he could think of was food. His new friend did not seem to have the same need and acted like he was going to keep on walking and talking with Ray. Ray told the man he could not go on; he had to have food and asked the man if he had any money to buy nourishment. A quick shake of his clothes and a few words convinced Ray that this man truly had not a penny. He told Ray that he was just a beggar who gave alms. Gave alms? Ray thought beggars received alms. Ray wondered when this guy had ever given alms. It appeared to Ray that it had been a long time since he had even seen money.

The man did, however, say that he knew where they could get a meal. He turned to the right of the road and climbed a set of stairs leading to a roof-top patio. There sat a table covered by a large awning. On the table sat a rustic looking loaf of bread, a dark bottle, and two stone glasses. Ray had hoped his first meal in this country would be more exciting, but quickly realized that he was in no position to choose. He resigned himself to eating what was offered. A small plate with oil on it was there beside the bread. Had it always been there?

Ray was about to work up the courage to ask the man his name but this thought was interrupted by the next words that came from the mouth of the man. He looked up into the sky, lifted the bread and cup and said, "Let he who is thirsty come and let he who is hungry eat, amen." With that he broke the loaf of bread into halves. Ray felt something like contact lenses fall out of his eyes and wondered if he would still be able to see. When he looked back at his host, he could indeed see clearly. Ray could see exactly who the man was.

17. The Beginning

His robe, which now looked like it had been dyed with the reddest of wine, fit him more tightly and it appeared that the man had grown a foot taller. His eyes glowed an eerie red and Ray thought that this same glow was coming from a spot on the man's chest as if something inside was on fire. His hands still looked injured but there was a nobility about them like the hands of a long-venerated king. A sword was slung low on the left hip of the man, and the hilt appeared to have seen many battles. Ray now knew that he must refer to the man as a king. Ray looked once more into the face of this man and into those remarkable eyes. In that face he saw a whole universe of emotions, yet only the good emotions of life. In that face, Ray saw love: the truest love he had ever known.

The King poured two glasses of wine. The aroma filled the air and seemed to tug at every sense of Ray's body. He felt that he could actually hear the smell of the wine. Ray had never really developed an appreciation for wine, but this one tugged at his soul and he craved its taste long before it came close to his lips.

They ate bread and drank wine in silence. The bread was the richest, tastiest, most wonderful bread he had ever tasted. Could it even be called bread? There were flavour notes that suggested roasted meats and dark spices of far-off lands. The wine could not be described and yet Ray's mind tried to capture the flavours as best it could. It reminded him of the buzzing of bees over a field of alfalfa, of freshly washed clothes on a line in the heat of summer, and of the dusky smell of evening-scented stalks. His mind was overwhelmed with joy and satisfaction.

Then the King asked Ray again what he had been thinking about when they had first seen each other on the road. Ray's mood changed. Ray realized that although they had spoken of a great many other things, they had not spoken of the truck, the pills, or the murders that had been committed. Ray's mind could not quite clear enough to answer the question that now came to mind. Why had he thought "murders?" Was it murder or murders that had been committed?

Ray told the King that he had been thinking about how he had been murdered by a member of his own family. He was wondering how to forgive that person. The King said that Ray was right in assuming that forgiveness and truth-telling were important. In fact, the King said, "Forgiveness cannot thrive where untruth is alive." The King asked for more detail. Who had killed him? Ray was hesitant to say more. He wanted to say something like he had heard in those TV stories about how he chose to remain silent for fear that he would incriminate himself. The internal struggle continued. Who was it that had killed him? Well, first he had to decide who he was himself. Was Ray the good guy or the bad guy in this TV series? Was he the victim or the accused? Indeed, he was both, and eventually that was how he answered. He told the King that he was the victim of death by pills and that he should be accused of causing the death. The King asked Ray if he could say this more plainly. "More plainly?" Ray had just answered as plainly as he could. He was no longer hiding anything from this King. Was this King less intelligent than he thought? Could he not understand what Ray was saying?

It occurred to Ray that perhaps this King did understand and it was Ray, himself, who had not spoken the whole truth. Who was the victim? Who was the accused? Then, as if a dam had burst, the story flowed out in one long saga. Ray barely took time to breathe. He started with the last few days of his life and told of how he had been discouraged and depressed about not having had work for over two years. He told of the financial problems, the collector cars he had to sell, the downsizing from a house to a tiny apartment, the cheap food and cheaper booze he had been eating and drinking, the truck speeding through the rural roads, the desolate well-site where he had made his decision, the loneliness and isolation, the friends who had left him, the wealthy friends who had looked at him with blank stares, and the family members who pitied seeing

him in this low estate. Then he began to recount
the rest of his life. He told of the accident with
Lydia, the cover-up. He told of years of living in
hiding – hiding all he knew about himself from
any who would seek to know him. He told of
being a horrible husband. He told of his failures
with his son, his daughter-in-law, his
granddaughter. He told of his disgust with
himself and how it had led him to a lonely road
and a desolate well-site. He told of how he had
taken his own life. He pushed away the bread and
wine and shouted, "I should not be sitting at this
table. Tell me to go away. Oh, I am lost."

Then, for what seemed like half an hour -
there was silence.

The King spoke first and this time he did not
call him friend; he called Ray a son. "My son, I
was aware of all of this before we ever spoke. I
know everything there is to know about you. You
are not condemned. You are forgiven. Yes, you
have broken the deep laws of the universe, but
there are deeper laws that you do not know.
Those laws are now at work in your life. You have
repented. My hands have broken your curse like I
broke this bread. The red fire in my eyes has
taken away your penalty. All is well."

Ray was full of questions. How could this be?
How could this be happening? How could this
King take away Ray's guilt? Ray's dirt? Ray's
murder? Ray's deception? Many of his questions
could not even be spoken, so he started thinking

of easier questions. The first question that he voiced to the King was about time. Ray asked how long it had been since he had died in the truck. The answer took him aback. The King told him that it had been about two Earth hours since Ray had taken the mouth full of pills. Back on Earth, his body was not yet dead. The last ebb of life was just leaving his pain-wracked body. Ray said, "Um, no, you must have misunderstood me. I have been in this place for months, perhaps years. I had all that time in space, a bunch of time on Venus, more time in this place. You and I have been together for several hours. I was asking how long it had been since my body floated out of the truck."

The King had a look of amusement in his eyes and said, "Two hours. Time in this place runs in a manner strange to that on earth. Time here can go forward, backward, sideways, slow, and fast. It can be very disorienting to those who have not experienced it before."

Ray could now sense it. His body was indeed still alive. All that had occurred had happened within the framework of his earthly life. His 57 years on earth and here in this place was one long ribbon of time. Some of it had gone by slowly and some of it had flown by incredibly fast. It all made sense now. He also realized that all the decisions he had made, like those related to the Collector on the Mountain, Matthew Sunday, Siddhartha, the Fountain, and the King, had been made within his lifespan. He was thankful that his life had ended with these choices made.

He spoke to the King about regret. He told him he felt bad that he had not made these decisions earlier in his life. He now realized all the joy and opportunities he had missed. The King looked at him with simultaneous sorrow and joy and said, "Yes, there are consequences to the life you lived. The darkness nearly took over completely. Yes, you nearly missed out. You could have come sooner. I sent several of my messengers to your home, work, and family. I sent several types of communications. The messages were all rejected or ignored. There were moments when it seemed you would certainly be lost. Even your last 30 minutes of life in this world were fragile. We thought we might lose you. But you are here now, so let us rejoice!"

Ray looked at the table again and saw that it had become larger and was filled with a whole new selection of food and drink. Ray had never seen such a banquet. There were fruits and vegetables, meats and cheeses, creamy desserts, a variety of wines and milk to drink. There were strawberries the size of Ray's head that tasted sweeter and juicier than any Ray had experienced. There were blueberries the size of strawberries, there were apples, oranges, bananas, cantaloupes, pumpkins, squash, and pears. Then there were the fruits that Ray could not even name: three-lobed apple-like creations, purple raspberry-like fruits, and other things Ray could not even describe. The meats and cheese were equally diverse. How many types of cheese could there be in this world? All of them were delicious. Despite being a picky eater in his former life, Ray found the flavour of every single item to be more than what he could have expected. He could not get enough of these wonderful foods.

Other people began to arrive at their private roof-top patio. The King got up from the table and greeted each person as they arrived. The people arriving were filled with such warmth for Ray that he too felt that he should be at the top of the stairs to greet the new arrivals. For a while, it became difficult to eat the magnificent food set before him. Ray was constantly jumping up to greet another person. He was pretty sure that these people were the messengers to whom the King had referred. There was the paper boy, not very good at hitting the porch with the newspaper, but always kind to his brother as he took him to baseball practice after he finished the deliveries. Ray was surprised to find himself giving the boy a big hug. Ray had never been much of a hugger, but seeing the enthusiasm of the guests and the King, it seemed like the right thing to do. There was that minister who kept coming by and asking for donations for the Boy Scouts. The Scouts only used the church building as their meeting place and the minister only fund-raised for them, but he did suggest that Ray could fund the entire Boy Scout Troop. Ray always found that this minister arrived at inconvenient times and in the past, Ray had been quite abrupt with him. Now here was Ray welcoming him with a handshake and one-armed hug. There was the pipe major from the local drum and bagpipe band. Ray had once been rather cruel and suggested that he could make better music by resuscitating an octopus. The pipe major simply invited Ray to bring his octopus to their next show and gave him two free tickets, assuring Ray that the "pet" would not need the second ticket. Ray greeted him and apologized profusely for his bad behaviour. The pipe major looked Ray square in the eyes and said, "Think nuthin' of it, young feller. Let us not waste any more time thinking of such things. Do ye think it matters here? Ach-noo!" There was the baker from the bakery Ray had loved to visit. They made the most marvelous cinnamon buns, so much like his mother's recipe that he wondered if they had stolen it from her. The baker was still wearing her ornate cross around her neck and kissed it before each sip of wine. There were too many messengers for Ray to count and he could now see that each of these people had played a role in his life and had indeed shown him a portion of the puzzle that made up this King. After what seemed like hours of getting up and down, Ray and the rest of the guests sat down and feasted for a long time. It seemed to Ray that they feasted for days, but Ray now knew that he could not trust his own sense of time in this place. Whatever the time, Ray and the guests felt it was just right.

He felt foolish, ridiculous, and obstinate for having ignored these wonderful people in the past, but everyone around the table was in good spirits. Everyone was raising a glass, or fork, in toast to Ray. Their eyes sparkled, they laughed, and clapped Ray on the back. They joked about killing the fatted calf and feasting until the sun went down, even as they all knew that the sun would never set in this land.

Eventually the feast did end. The guests all said goodbye and made their way to other places until Ray and the King were once more alone. Ray wondered what was next but he was afraid to ask. The King simply rose from the table and made a follow-me motion with his head. Ray asked, "Where are we going?" The King gave a wink and said, "Farther up, and further in." Ray did not exactly know what that would mean, but the smile on both of their faces convinced him that it would most certainly be good. Ray was ready for a new adventure. He sprang to his feet and raced the King down the stairs. The stone pavement below felt like Swiss cheese beneath his feet and the air was soft and warm. He realized he had left his shoes underneath the table upstairs. He did not return for them.

As Ray and the King carried on down the road, they stopped at a high lookout. From this point, Ray could see back over vast stretches of where he had been. There was the Fountain; there was Siddhartha's temple and the black stone; all of Venus was laid out before him. He could see the people with whom he had engaged since he had arrived in this other-land. The two sat for what seemed like a long time and looked at the various things going on in these worlds. Ray found the boundary between the life he lived on earth and the two hours he had spent in this world blurring together. How many of the incidents on Venus were things he had experienced in his 57 years on earth? How much had he tried to find God in life? In death? When had he repented? How could he be forgiven for all that he had done? Was this the real world or the life he had known before? It was all beginning to scramble in his mind. For a while he tried to keep it all straight. Soon he realized it just didn't matter. All of his life had been an endless series of choices and paths. Most of the time, he had made the wrong choices and taken the wrong paths; by the King's grace, he had taken just enough right paths.

Ray began to wonder about all the people he could still see: the Collector with her mountain of stuff, the man sitting by his tree, Matthew Sunday and the beautiful women, Siddhartha, the Fountain companions, the woman in the fort. What was their fate? Ray raised his eyes to the King and began to say something. Before he could ask, the King said, "Their journey is their journey; their life is not your life; and their journey and their life is not yet over. There are no questions that can yet be answered about these people." Again they sat quietly for a few minutes. Ray was lost in thought as both joy and sadness welled up

in his soul. He longed to know the answer to the
question of who else would make it to this place
with this King. He knew he could not
ask. He dared not ask for fear of rousing a stern
look from this King.

Finally the King rose and said, "All right
then, here we go, farther up and further in." Ray
did venture one question, "When will I see
clearly? I feel as if I can see a little more than I
used to see, but not nearly as much as I need."
The King smiled a knowing smile and said that
one day all would be clear. "For now, I suggest
you focus on the hem of my cloak." Ray had not
seen it before, but now it came clearly into focus.
The hem of the King's garment looked to be sewn
with thread made of the purest of gold.
Suddenly, that was enough for now. Ray
continued on.

ABOUT THE AUTHOR

Keith Shields has studied science and theology most of his adult life and has a Bachelor of Science in Molecular Biology, a Bachelor of Religious Education, and a Master of Arts in Theology. He writes songs as one half of the duo known as Key of Zed and he is employed as a pastor at Bow Valley Christian Church in Calgary. His wife, Maureen, and he have three adult daughters who each have children of their own. He is hopeful that one day his grandchildren may read *The Great Beyond*.